Fire Road

The

John

Simmons

Short

Fiction

Award

University of

Iowa Press

Iowa City

*Donald
Anderson*

*Fire
Road*

University of Iowa Press, Iowa City 52242

Printed in the United States of America

http://www.uiowa.edu/~uipress

The publication of this book was generously supported by the
University of Iowa Foundation and the National Endowment
for the Arts.

Printed on acid-free paper

Library of Congress Cataloging-in-Publication Data

Anderson, Donald, 1946 July 9–

    Fire road / by Donald Anderson.

         p.   cm.—(The John Simmons short fiction award)

      ISBN 0-87745-778-6 (pbk.)

        1. United States—Social life and customs—

20th century—Fiction.   I. Title.   II. Series.

PS3601.N54 F5   2001

813'.6—dc21   2001033589

01 02 03 04 05 P 5 4 3 2 1

For E

It is all practice: when we emerge

from experience we are not wise

but skillful. But at what?

—ALBERT CAMUS

. . . we don't have to live great lives,

we just have to understand and survive

the ones we've got.

—ANDRE DUBUS

Contents

ACKNOWLEDGMENTS

Some of the stories in this volume were first
published elsewhere, sometimes in an altered
form: "Twenty Ways to Look at Fire,"
"Quotidian," "sab·o·tage," and "Endnotes"
in *Fiction International*; "Wonder Bread"
and "The Art of Fiction" in *PRISM
international*; "Weather" and "Luck" in
Epoch; "Scaling Ice" in *sub-TERRAIN*;
"mav·er·ick" in *ASYLUM Annual
1994*; "Fathers" and "Bliss" in *Western
Humanities Review*; "My Name Is Stephen
Mann" in *Aethlon*; "Accident" in *Weber
Studies*; "The Peacock Throne" in *Columbia*;
"Fire Road" in *Short Story*; "Would You
Feel Better?" in *Connecticut Review*; "The
End of Times" in *Sniper Logic*; and "Baby
Teeth" in the *North American Review*,
reprinted in *aftermath: an anthology of
post-vietnam fiction*, reprinted here by
permission of Henry Holt and Co., Inc.;
"Overpass," an excerpt from "Barrie Hooper's
Dead" in the *North American Review*.
I am indebted to the story "Meeting You,"
from *Let Us Know* by Diane Vreuls, for the
context of the dream in "Epilogue"; to
Mission with LeMay: My Story by General
Curtis E. LeMay with MacKinlay Kantor,
for the quotations which appear in
"sab·o·tage"; to the *Gazette-Telegraph*,
which ran a want-ad column entitled
"Maverick." Other less extended quotations
are referenced in the text to their authors.
I wish to express my appreciation to the
National Endowment for the Arts for its
Creative Writers' Fellowship Grant and
to the Iowa Writers' Workshop and the
University of Iowa Press for their stubborn
support of the short story.

Fire Road

My
Name
Is
Stephen
Mann

Aboard a troopship from Calais to New York, after the Great War, my grandfather Arthur said he'd made up his mind to get rich. "Got it stuck in my nut to get rich. *Alaska.*"

In the lunar landscape of Mormon Utah, Arthur hailed his father, but Johann refused to stake a northern search for mere gold—*earthly gold*—though he offered Arthur, his youngest, a son's share of the farm in exchange for work. "Godly toil," Bishop Mann pronounced. "Fruitful labor."

"Shook my father's hand," Arthur said, "then I turned to tramp east. I turned to track down Jack Dempsey. I unloaded on him; he unloaded on me. A piece of action costs. I should know." Arthur meant the browned teeth on the night table in the saucer.

These teeth he'd saved did look as if they'd been snapped at the gum line, just as Arthur explained, not loosened. The dried teeth had no weight, but when I cupped the six in my palm, I'd pretend they made my hand sink.

"Spoiled my smiler," Arthur said, "but he staked me."

Arthur had told me his stories. I knew about the futile search for gold, knew about the Dempsey stake—the cherished snapped teeth—the hard trudge to Alaska (the harder trudge home), the two-year moose diet, the amazing weather.

Arthur pointed at the teeth. "Three months with the champ, but he staked me."

In 1919, Jack Dempsey was training to fight Jess Willard. My grandfather claimed Jack fought that fight—the World's Heavyweight Championship Fight—with cracked ribs. "Jack hired me to harden his body," Arthur said. "What I did was crack his ribs. The ribs was cracked when he went in to fight Jess. I cracked 'em."

I believed my grandfather had been a better fighter than he said. "You cracked Jack's ribs," I said whenever he told the story. A singer in his church, I sang: "You cracked 'em."

"Outweighed, *one*," Arthur said, "outreached, *there's two*, busted up with his own broke ribs," he said, fanning the fingers of a hand, keeping count, "that's *three*—Jack almost murdered Jess."

Years after when I checked the facts, I found Arthur had reported the truth. The Jess Willard Jack Dempsey destroyed had been a giant: the tallest boxing champion of all time. The writers wrote no boxing king had ever been so dethroned.

Jack clubbed Jess to the canvas seven times in the first round, then clubbed him for two rounds more. When the bell rang for round four, Willard couldn't respond. His jaw was broken, his left cheek was smashed, his right ear pulped and permanently deafened. The ribs housing Willard's lungs sagged like belts. In the end, Willard couldn't see the blows. Jack'd punched Willard's eyes shut. Jack Dempsey. The champion my grandfather slugged for three months. Jack—fifty-eight pounds lighter, five inches shorter, outreached by six—had all but murdered Jess.

Willard couldn't answer the bell. The nerve lines from his brain to his legs and to his arms were down. Under a hellish sun—120 degrees ringside—Willard's fists hung like sacked flour. Willard couldn't see, breathe, hear, spit. He couldn't stand. He couldn't lift his fists.

I looked up pictures of the match. Jack's sunburned arms look machined, bolted on: the arms of a man who could wreck you. Willard lasted three rounds with Jack. My grandfather lasted three months. Every day, Arthur and Jack punched each other.

"Jack bombed on me," Arthur said.

"You bombed him."

"I bombed him."

Arthur claimed he'd watched Dempsey straighten a horseshoe with his hands. Arthur swung his bare feet from the bed, over the side of his bed to the floor, then thrust his clenched fists toward me, then pulled, straightening the imaginary **U** to a bar.

"You saw it," I said.

Arthur placed his hands again into the empty air before him. He grunted, then pulled on the **U**.

"You saw it."

"I threw terrible rights," confided Arthur. "I was terrible to the body." But Arthur meant terrible as in *TERRIBLE* rights. *Heart-breaking* rights. *Bone-breaking.*

"Drank my own hooch," my grandfather said, "knew where it was made and who made it." Arthur raised his half glass of Jim Beam to better catch the light from his window. Arthur studied the commercial booze, sighting through. "Not this. No chemical. Just the natural pure growth of corn." Arthur lowered his glass without drinking. With his bridges out, my grandfather looked as I believed Willard looked after Dempsey smashed him.

"How old?"

My grandfather knew, but I said it: "Fourteen."

"You had a cooker and a cooler," my grandfather said, "a *condenser*. If you ever saw a still, what you'd see is two parts. You'd see the cooker, here," he said—the whiskey hopped from his glass—"then you'd see your worm run from the cooker to the condenser, here. The condenser condenses the steam. It has to be cooled as it goes. Liquid," Arthur said. "*Hooch.* You boil it off and you make it. My still was good copper. No bad buckets—no zinc, no lead. No adulteration. I never used sugar even if it was cheaper to do it. Shouldn't tell you."

"Tell me."

"I could tell you things," he said.

"Tell me."

"Drink enough of something, you get sick of it."

The summer I turned fourteen was the summer my father, Harry, and I grubbed out our basement, from beneath our house that already stood. My grandfather had moved in with us, and we needed the room. Before winter, we'd finished my basement bedroom and a storeroom for food. We'd hauled down a freezer to that room and stocked shelves with canned food as though my father had been warned of war or famine. We had rinsed-out Clorox bottles of water I switched out fresh every month. We had blankets and towels and matches, flashlights, batteries, coats, sweaters, a whetstone. We had bullets. We had bottles of aspirin. We had Vitamin C.

We had two rooms to go. When we were done with the basement, the plan was to extend the kitchen and construct indoor stairs. Meantime, I had to go outside to get to my room. I'd lift the cellar door to climb down the rungs of a ladder. Before I'd lower the door on my head for the night, I'd cut the outside light and sort among the stars for motion. I was looking for Sputnik.

Snow on the cellar door made it weigh. I'd lower the door, then climb on a stool. I pumped that door. I wanted bludgeon arms, bull shoulders.

I played trumpet in my school's summer band, and one of our songs, "Melody of Love," was my grandfather's favorite. I'd raise my Conn to my lips—sunstruck and windy brass through Arthur's opened windows, dishes of half-eaten custard on the sills, half bottles of booze, morning sun gilding through.

Beyond the window ran a field of cheat grass and untended iris. And beyond the field, one of Butte's old smelter dumps.

Anaconda had long since closed its Butte smelters, but the slag stuck. All my life, I heard how Pittsburgh Glass was transferring workers from its eastern plants to Montana to take a crack at Butte's slag, to remelt it for windows.

My grandfather squinted to look beyond the field of iris and grass. He said that the slag looked like black wax, melted candles. Then he moved a hand towards the sill, jabbed a bottle. Arthur Mann was a drunk. His bottles were out. He didn't hide them.

Pittsburgh never got around to sending workers or hiring ours after our smelters shut down, or even later when the mines closed. Outside my grandfather's window was always the slag, piled high on itself and unflowing, black as tires, guarding glass.

Arthur said he was a one-handed fighter. "No left," he said. "You can't beat a champ with one hand, just chumps." When he said *no left*, my grandfather balled his right hand to a fist, then raised it. The arm was unmuscled—the TERRIBLE right—bone and draped skin.

"When you're old enough to drink with me," Arthur said, "I'll be gone. Play that melody," he said. "*That* song."

I'd play the song for him. My grandfather's song. I'd play it.

In the basement Harry and I dug, I lay in my bed in the dark beneath my grandfather's room and envisioned him boiling *hooch*. I didn't then know that his nineteen-year-old partner, Ezra Young, had been caught at the still and had taken bullets in the chest and what seemed a stray one through the eye. The hole where the slug left Ezra's head was not the size of a surprised blue eye, but a shoe. It was a hole you could have slipped your foot through. That's what my father, Harry, said when he produced a picture postcard he said had been made up at the time to be sold to tourists. In the old card's dark tints, Ezra Young is roped to a board and the board is propped up for the photo. Two revenuers and a Mormon sheriff pose in hats in the shot. The two Feds had signed their names in legible script, black ink: Vaughn Koch and Robert Morgan. Between them, Ezra Young looks plattered, a prize trout.

My name is Stephen Mann. I was born in 1946, one consequence of Armistice. My father, Harry, would have served had he
not caught a wood chip in an eye in his father's wood yard, blind-
ing him enough to disqualify him for war. He was touched by the
loss of battle anyhow: his best friend, Lovell, sinking with the
Utah.

Harry married after the attack on Pearl Harbor and Lovell's
memorial service—in photos: an empty, flagged casket—but refused to sire children until treaties had been signed, and what
must have seemed the final drop of atomic bombs.

My father, who would have planted his feet and tracked a bomb
from high skies to his shoes, was afraid of water and horses.
Arthur had owned the wood yard that had one-eyed his son, and
Harry remembered the horses harnessed to snake out timber.
My father had been bitten and thrown. He'd been stepped on. If
we were together and saw a horse, my father wouldn't let me
get near it. He enrolled me, though, in Red Cross swimming. In
1940, his dead best friend had signed with the Navy without
learning a stroke.

My father went through the business about the attack on
Pearl Harbor. "Water burned. Johnny Weismuller couldn't've
swum it." Harry still missed Lovell. "If you don't thank me now,
you will," Harry said. "You can learn to swim," he said. "You
have to."

I said I wanted to learn to swim.

"That's fine," he said. "You have to."

What I know now is that whatever would have happened to my
father in World War II would have happened to him five years before my birth. He'd wanted to sign up with Lovell. In 1940, in
Butte, Montana, recruiters were teaming up pals for sea duty
shipmates.

The things my father did best made noise. When a tree
crashed, he'd praise himself aloud, his ax work proud and safe as
music. When my father's ax struck, it launched chunks that skied
heavy as ore, then thudded like nuggets.

The first summer I was allowed to use an ax was the same summer I learned to swim. I learned that summer, too, to stretch barbed wire, to slaughter and dress pigs, to countersink nails, to jump-start a car, to solder.

All the summers I hadn't been allowed to swing an ax in my father's inherited wood yard, my father had me help him saw. I established myself on my side of things to grasp the saw's tall handle. Harry would have filed and set the teeth just as his father, Arthur, had taught him. Harry oiled the wood handles of his saw as Mother oiled wood in the parlor.

I see him still—my father on his side of things—sawdust plastering his arms. Sawdust smacking his teeth. I see him spit and grin. My father had his father's fighter arms—his saw pushed through wood like a song.

Harry's birthday was this week. He said he felt well. "*Fit*," is how he put it. Then: "*Chipper*, except for the cancer. *Liver*, but stomach sounds better. I call it stomach for your mother." Then he told me what I knew: liver cancer had killed his father. "That, and hooch. Oh, Arthur," he said.

I sat at the phone with my eyes shut. My father went on. He never swallowed liquor in his life, which accounted, he said, for the years. He addressed the five-year death difference between him now and his father at the time of that death as if it were a won race. Then he said I should have seen Arthur. "You knew him," he said, "as a drunk. My pals would tag home with me just to see him, to watch him saw wood or to load it. My father was a god," Harry said. "You don't know."

Thirty years ago I asked my grandfather if I was more like him or like my father. I asked after I'd donned my grandfather's boxing gloves and had just floored my shadow. I was boxing for Arthur in his room just before he left our house for the County Home. I was sixteen, my grandfather sixty-seven. My grandfather was, in fact, dying, but what did I know of that?—I was wearing his boxing gloves with his permission. I'd never before stuffed my fists into his mitts in his presence.

"I'm like you," I said, then swung up my gloved dukes to prove it. I'd just stepped back from my shadow on the wall to a neutral corner. "I'm more like you than I'm like my father."

"What you live is your life," Arthur said.

After my father hung up, I started to call back. Instead, I sat by the phone, gulped bourbon.

Arthur Mann professed no middle name, as though the act made him mysterious and essential. To explain: *Babe Ruth. Abe Lincoln. Joe Louis. Jesus Christ,* he pointed out. *Jack Dempsey.*

Before he was twenty-five, Arthur Mann had staked gold claims in Alaska where he discovered no gold but lucked through two winters on moose meat. The summer he turned twenty-five, my grandfather hiked home from the Yukon. He had a world war under his belt. He'd stepped in and out of boxing rings. He'd fought the record cold of two Yukon winters and had had the strength to hump home.

There's a photo of Arthur on his arrival home that summer. In the photo, Arthur looks strong and as unknowing as anyone must be to create a life, to move toward devils and decision and loss. In the photo, my grandfather is a picture of prospect and goal. He doesn't look fooled. The photo, snapped in 1921, shows Arthur beside his father. Great-Grandfather Johann Wallisch Mann wears a tar black suit. His high white collar looks stiff as fear or faith.

When I studied the photo, I'd look at my grandfather's face, then at mine in a mirror, then compare both to his fabled Mormon father, Bishop Mann. In the year of the photo, Johann, aged one hundred, stands erect. His tall posture seems a trick, like the stick wrists that poke beyond his sleeves. It is as though, even at his age, Johann could have outboxed his son by merely lifting his fists.

In the photo, Arthur sports a steam-creased black hat. When study the image now, I see that Arthur looks bemused and a ease. And why not? A man who has survived head-deep snow and temperatures fully ninety degrees below freezing, Arthur basks in the sun in Utah. His hat is cocked.

My grandfather has unbuttoned his cuffs and rolled his sleeves His arms, next to his father's unending stick wrists, look godly proportioned. Forty years before his death, my grandfather arms look perfect. Even when I was young, I sensed my grand-father—*this* grandfather in the photo—had surely considered the world not only as large and wide, but as conspicuously fit for plunder.

It's a day's drive from where Arthur slouches in the photo to the foothills, to the claims where in place of drill and pick work he and Ezra cooked the hooch they then sold to pale, failed Saints, tall Ute warriors, and squaws I pictured with buckskinned hips as willing as saddles.

In my father's version of his father's whiskey business success, Harry and his sister, Ramona, are the only children in Vernal, Utah, with new shoes. The story isn't true because Arthur had yet to marry. My father, Harry, hadn't been born. When I was old enough to apply the math of time against Harry's story, he ignored me.

Arthur lived in our house. He was the man who told me stories and who guarded a pair of old boxing gloves he hung on the wall by his bed. The gloves were thin as winter mittens. They would have hardly cushioned a blow. Time had cracked the leather. Twisted right, I thought, either glove could have split flesh. They could have opened a face. Though I never saw him with them on, my grandfather kept the gloves within reach, as though ready for business.

On the day Arthur died, I ran to his room in our house for the teeth, the collection of six that had been snapped with punches. In all my life I'd never seen the saucer on the night table empty. I ran to my father to report this, but as soon as I started, I knew. I said I wanted the teeth. I demanded the teeth. My father, Harry, said no.

Into the grave I dropped the armload of iris I'd torn from the field across the road from Arthur's window—the window where he piled his dirty spoons and cups, the window where he'd stored his bottles, the window from where he looked beyond the purple iris he called flags at the slag that the men from Pittsburgh never came for.

Through the springs and summers Arthur lived with us, the number of flags between his window and the slag multiplied as though someone had been faithfully sowing, but the slag still governed the field like a dark glacier that had ceased its motion. I came to see the slag as an ice-numbed foul mound that in time, under sun, might reveal its treasure. I imagined gold that had been planed from the earth and transported from my grandfather's Yukon to his own back door. But whatever precious earth the black slag had borne had been stripped: fired then frozen for metal: copper, lead, zinc. But always the taste and the hope for gold. Destruction for gold. Slag piled on slag. Enduring and abandoned. Vain and inane and sterile.

The year Arthur died, the iris appeared unusually profuse and bright. Arthur had proposed that rain rinsing off the slag had been spreading a welcomed erosion of dust—lava dust—magma tonic for growth.

Arthur said, "I could tell you things."

I probably wanted to tell him I loved him, but I was sixteen. What I said was, "That crap's not dissolvable dust, it's glass rock." I said that the slag was useless, that it couldn't even be crushed for fill or for roads. I said it would puncture tires.

———

The sky for the funeral had cleared of clouds and looked domed. The color above was a paled violet, as though it were the hour for sunrise or new snow.

I cradled Arthur's flags. In the day's light wind the petals flapped like gills. In my pocket were the teeth I'd scooped from a drawer in my father's dresser.

Soil clung to the uprooted flags, the dried bulbs and the tubers. The dirty roots looked as haggard as the leaves and the bloom looked new. I dropped Arthur's flags in the hole, then stepped to the edge. The purple blooms of the flags looked vague and frail and showy, but the hard green leaves shone like swords.

"Kill the body, the head dies," Arthur informed me on the day he left our house for the County Home. He was quoting Joe Louis. This conversation was the last we would start in his room. From the side of his bed, on this last day in his room, Arthur Mann attempted to stand. He caught his breath, then still sitting, raised his arms. He threw unballed fists in my direction, like slow ghost fish at my ribs. I raised my elbows, then dropped them in to be guards. I warded off his phony blows. I worked in slow motion too. Elbows in place, I moved a fake hook toward Arthur's left side. I had to bend to do it—Arthur's head was below my chin—but my ducking move to the ribs seemed to make my grandfather happy, though he dropped his hands and grimaced. "Can the head," he said. "It moves," he said. "Bomb the gut."

In two weeks, Arthur would die. "You can change your luck," he said, "if you hard bang the body. Bomb the gut." Arthur drew a breath, then placed a hand on my hip to steady. I hadn't guessed at my grandfather's pain. In the privacy of his own company, Arthur Mann had been falling apart.

"I was beautiful to the body," he said. "You too." But he said it too loud. He lifted his hand from my hip to reach to the wall for the gloves. "Be beautiful," he said. "You, too."

I gingered my hands into my grandfather's gloves. I didn't look up to confirm the permission. Mitts on, I stared at my fists. I felt dangerous. Along the cracks in the gloves ran slivers of a color like rust, as if it were blood and not time that had broken the leather.

Turned toward the wall—toward my shadow—menacingly crouched, elbows tucked, rolling my shoulders, I fired thunderous hooks belly high. But with the gloves on my hands, the temptation proved too much, and I delivered a sneak right, then unloaded a crusher—a left to the exact, exposed point of the imaginary jaw above me, a jaw just as tall and as open as Willard's. Like Dempsey's tall man, mine crumpled. With Arthur's gloves on my hands, I'd floored him. I'd probably opened his face.

I straightened, glowered at my phantom man on the floor. My footwork had felt to me smooth by instinct, a blind man skirting ice. I believed I'd discovered Dempsey's rhythm.

My grandfather said Jack Dempsey lost his chance to regain his title for failing to retreat to the farthest neutral corner after flooring Gene Tunney: "And Tunney was *floored,* no mistake. Sixteen seconds. Jack *stands* over Gene for ten. *Goddamnit.*"

I stepped back from the wall.

Arthur said by the time Dempsey stopped hovering over Tunney and got to the neutral corner, Tunney'd gathered and hauled himself up. He stayed clear of the champ for the next three rounds, won on points. "Hell," Arthur said, "Jack was too old." In 1927, in an outdoor ring in Philadelphia, in a driving rain, King Jack was too old.

"Even the day before," Arthur said, "Goddamnit. Tunney wouldn't've lasted—not with Jack. Age'll catch you." In 1927, when age caught him, Jack Dempsey turned thirty-two.

It would not be surprising for anyone to think the split mitts I pulled on my fists two weeks before my grandfather died form my lasting image of him, but what I see are his feet: yellow nails that smelled of something like cigarette ash when I clipped them, or scorched fish, or what I thought would be the smell of a burning circus. Yellow nails. Yellow, crippled toes. As if Arthur's ravaged feet, after more than sixty years, could still bend to his mouth like a baby's. As if, in that position and ambifooted, he'd smoked all his life. Cigarettes between toes, toe flesh callusing to flake like mica. Or gold. Discolored gold. Finally, gold. Dirty canary stains. Veins. Lucky Strikes. He loved me.

Quotidian

Reading the Paper:

1. You are an Egyptian merchant on holiday on the Nile. There is an explosion in the bow of your ship and the stored fuel ignites. In an attempt to save your life, you strip then leap into the water, but it is spring and the Nile is high and muddy, and the crocodiles hunt.

2. Or you are female, Swiss, on holiday in Japan, admiring the northern coast, and are washed—no warning—from its shore. In the seconds granted you for fear, you think not of buildings collapsing inland in the cities. You think of yourself, and of the children and their nun sitting quietly in sand, each child grasping a prize of kelp and shell. You had photographed the children—

the thin nun nodding yes—who sat for you, sober-faced and happy.

You are photographed yourself, hours after final tremors, face-down in the surf, beside a floating roof from the children's village. This moment, shot from the air—color by Fuji—flashes about the world, garners awards. You become a symbol of disaster.

3. Or this: A local twenty-six-year-old has been arraigned.

He picks up a female high school senior, drives her to a parking lot. Then, forcing her into the back of his windowless van, dons a pair of red boxing gloves and informs the girl he will punch her silly unless she disrobes. The girl undresses to her underclothes. The twenty-six-year-old—still wearing the gloves—removes the girl's underwear then violates her without permission.

"Violates her? Violates without permission?" Abby Lutz cries from her office. You have arrived at work and just sat at your desk when she storms into the hallway, brandishing the morning news, knocking on closed doors. "Goddamnit, say rape. You can't say it? RAPE!"

The twenty-six-year-old, employed by Hewlett-Packard, the reporter reports, speaks Arabic, invents computer circuits, and in pleading *nolo contendere*, claims illegal confiscation of his red leather mitts.

All morning the office percolates. Women's voices. Men's voices: "Boxing gloves?" "Oh, Ho!" "Ah Ha!" Late in the day, tiny Abby rises from her chair in the executive lounge to face Earl Howe. All day, Earl Howe has been ragging Abby about sex and mittens, something about lost mittens. He does it again then sits back in his chair. Earl Howe thinks the story about the boxing gloves is funny. Abby Lutz punches Earl in the nose. (The blow occurs so fast, you are not later certain whether it was an open palm or fist.) Earl's nose inflates. The pig flow of blood seems a trick.

Buying Groceries:

Park to walk into a grocery. Pass a stalled red truck: an old Dodge blotched with an off-color rust, as though pelted with spoiled cherries. A woman lolls behind the wheel, smoking a Parliament

The pretty woman's dog sits patiently in the back of the unsided, flatbed truck. The truck's load is strapped down. The dog sits atop treated fence posts. There's a keg of zinc-coated staples, eight rolls of zinc-coated barbed wire, and a long-handled tool to string the wire without slicing your tightened fists.

The dog is wearing a baseball cap which has been adjusted for his head. The cap reads: *Bama Feed*. You would have expected the woman to have been listening to music.

Now, driving home with your bags of food, you pass an unmet neighbor who, in the three weeks since he's arrived, you've never seen without cap and goggles and standing on a ladder scrubbing the sides of his house. He wears rubber gloves. The neighbor sees you and waves. His rubber hand steams, the yellow fingers.

Watching TV:

Raise the sound. Pour the drink. Chamber music since Korea. Chamber music from our times, with newsreel clips—timed video bursts—of the trouble at Kent State; Selma; the University of Mississippi. Jack Ruby plugging Oswald. Martin Luther King, last glimpses of; the text of his single-hearted song: His dream. Ours. Sputnik and bags from Nam. Smoke-ins; smoke-outs; boys prancing in the streets. Gloria Steinem switching her ass, *swit-swit*. Henry Fonda with his Oscar. Johnson and Nixon and Ford. Juan Corona, in the orchards in Yuba City, flagging graves. Lieutenant William Calley. The rise and fall of Haig. Yoko Ono's first solo album.

Face the old portable black-and-white. Remember the division of living cells you watched on "Mr. Wizard." Picture in your mind's eye Mr. Janey's ninth-grade science class: moving frames projected—from twenty-five years before—in irregular and aching light: the thermal winds of atomic detonation, the live twitch of a sprout of wheat, the flowering of rice, the rise of flattened cities.

Drink and wait (PBS moves on, signs off), then steer to your back porch to shout at the brilliant, unstarlit dark. Lift your rum in tribute to the lightning firing about the sky like brain waves, then pilot, dry-eyed, toward your room. When you think or dream of your daughter's mother, she is arriving from some foreign shore. She accuses in what sounds like Spanish.

At your child's closed door, again raise your drink: *Dommage*, you pronounce in French because you can. *Dommage.* In her sleep, your daughter, Alex, stirs. Cover your mouth with your hand. Your daughter's new pup bumps to the floor from the bed, investigates beneath the closed door, sniffing, as you stand and stand in the unlamped hall.

Wonder Bread

In the Pennsylvania Academy of Fine Arts were sculpted slices of bread, a leather valise, still lifes of pickup trucks and semis, and a canvas which faked a four-by-eight-foot panel of construction-grade plywood hammered to the wall. Across the gallery was a seated naked woman. *Red-Haired Woman, Green Velvet Chair* refocused your attention from the artist's technique—his *precision*—to her individual self. She was triumphantly and generously herself. Polyvinyl Truth.

Trace spied me at the plywood. She stood before her class and beside the naked woman. Even from where I stood, the nude sculpture appeared numbingly real. I checked the catalog: Fig. 129.

John DeAndras. 1979. Cast vinyl, polychromed in oil, life-size
Private collection. New York.

I strained to hear Trace speak to her college students. *Except
for the nude, what image pulls us all? What else would it be
bread? a porcelain tub? the Sphinx?* Then: *Sculpture occupie
space in a way a human can't.* You can stare at art, Trace said
She touched a hand to her hair, which was short in a calculate
way. I could picture Trace as a terrorist, clipped hair quick-dye
or slipped, slick as Teflon, into caps, nylons, wool masks.

When I saw Kent's Trace, I knew her. Another man's mistress
she was both more and less than I expected. She stood in a blac
sundress. She seemed intentionally untanned, and, like the *Red
Haired Woman,* appeared as illusion as well as fact: a cranking u
of special effects. I felt the urge to shift closer and stare. Which i
why I'd been invited on this pilgrimage east: I, Stephen Mann
was to be Kent's witness. My friend, Kent, had chosen me.

There was about Trace, in this place, the unbelabored dazzle o
a master pencil sketch. As a drawing, Trace might have been a
Dürer. But knowing what I did about Kent and Trace, any kind o
starchy pose struck as a thrilling ruse, a snare.

Kent was still outside, trying to park the rented car. He'
dropped me at the curb, convinced someone would free a meter
"I'm going in," I said, pointing at an attended parking advertising
space for three bucks. "Put it there."

To my mind, Kent seemed too cheerful, too expectant in hi
turning from his wife, June, to Trace. Kent seemed unscraped
The failure of my own marriage had undone me. Who was Ken
to escape?

Before and throughout my marriage, my wife, so it turned out
had slept with other men, though the first time Anna and I mad
love came late. Six days before the wedding, we were finally i
the sack, only to be interrupted by her landlord thumping on th
door. Anna answered the door in my shirt. She told the landlor
to stay put, then their voices lowered. I strained to hear then
talk. Anna returned to the bedroom, dropped my shirt, stood b
my side of her bed. *Do something,* she said. *It's cold.*

We lived in Montana; we lived in Utah; we moved to Omaha, Nebraska. We made Alexandra and Daniel—sister and brother—then lurched along. I was astonished to be so unhappy. At the end, Anna would refuse me in our bed. She would turn to me: *No*—ruffle her hand beneath the sheets—*but here, I can help you if you want.* Sometimes I told her yes.

After Anna moved out—taking baby Dan—my daughter and I soon moved to Colorado, from where I filed for divorce. Anna called from Omaha, amazed to have received the lawyer's notice. *You're a terribly selfish man. I doubt you can be cured.*

I'd moved to Colorado because a Boulder-based small press had accepted a batch of my work, and because, even in Nebraska, I felt I'd retreated too far east. I began work for Hewlett-Packard (technical writing) and waited for the birth of my book. My stories weren't published for months. Meantime, I wrote for Hewlett-Packard eight hours a day on a Hewlett-Packard computer. I wrote technical notes, instructions, warnings, Hewlett-Packard ads: "Computers for Life." At night I listened to a jazz station out of Denver. That year, I read all Alexandra's fourth-grade texts: her science, math, history, English—the works.

Colorado had seemed as good a spot to restart as most. When I'd gotten the contract for the book, I dug out a map, looked for Boulder. What do you do with a town that seems named as a western version of Plymouth Rock? I said the name of the state out loud: C-O-L-O-R-A-D-O. Then: *Denver, Golden, Aurora, Rush, Sangre de Cristo, Divide, Rifle, Cope, Fairplay, Last Chance, Loveland.*

"We're moving, Alex. To where we fit. The Rockies. Someplace solid."

Alexandra pointed out—something I'd read in her books—that the earth's surface (its crust, its peaks) shifted a full six feet, like oceans, every day.

"Do I care if mountains rise or fall if I don't see them do it?"

"Doesn't mean they don't, Steve," said Alex, employing my name to make the point.

"Well, now, Alex," I said, "there you are."

In Montana, as a child, I'd seen the sun rise and set with respect to eternal peaks. Colorado Springs, it turned out, had mountains only to the west.

When my stories were finally published, the printing run was small. I'd written about Mormons, miners, prizefighters, strikers, losers, dreamers, bums. If the stories were linked by idea, it was not that the West had been won, but that the rush to ruin is as ancient as it is abiding, and as common in Promised Lands as any. It was later I broached Skinny Fiction, Mini-Fiction, Sudden-, Flash-, Micro-, Snap-Fiction, the Short-Shorts my father thought tongue-tied, weak witted, disrespectful. *A respectable story is not fast food or a quickie divorce, and it certainly isn't an insurance form you need a priest to read, or whatever else you or anyone means these things to be.* Then he started in on something about attention spans and my giving into *this short business. What was wrong with your first book?*

I started to say that it wasn't that people didn't have attention spans, but that each new day made it harder to believe in a future. What I ended up saying was that short-shorts were easier to publish because they were short. *What?* my father said. *Diet Fiction?*

My first book sold to libraries with review copies to selected professors. Kent, a professor who read the book, wrote to me from across town to offer dinner then, later, arranged a job for me at his school. I quit Hewlett-Packard. Alex began sixth grade.

Kent and I were fast friends. And I liked June, the wife of twenty-five years he would leave for Trace. Kent's break from June hardly qualified as a surprise. Kent and June weren't ones to stage themselves just in private. I was in their home the night Kent announced to June his need for Trace: THE LEAVING

FADE IN:
INTERIOR—NIGHT

The camera pans KENT and JUNE's living room. The color of the room and its furniture (modern) is glossy white, though the room can hardly be described as neutral. The floor, for instance, so shiny it looks wet, is enamel black. There is good art on the walls. There are vases, wire and metal sculpture, rugs, bookcases (crammed), books scattered about—above all, it is a house where books are read. The room is lighted by torchière lamps. The light of each lamp is bright, but local—

thus, the room appears both over- and underlit. In the corners are stereo speakers the size of dwarfs.

The camera slows past color photographs of Kent and June. In these photos, Kent and June are young. Kent stands on a country club porch, peacocky, in a summer suit. The breeze has mussed his hair, but everything else is picture perfect: the shirt is hard starched, the shoes beam white, the necktie is snug at the collar.

June stands on grass. The sweater she wears in her photo is drawn across her chest as she draws a bow, arrow aimed at a target outside the frame. Her hair has been tied back. From the stretch of the sweater and tendons in her neck, you feel the strain of the pull for June. A different view of the clubhouse rises behind June, though the building here is obscured by flowering hedges, small trees. June, at once, blooms and looks as though she could hold the bowstring taut forever.

The camera arrests at the glass-topped dining table. The glass top is a smoky gray. The china, like the floor, honest black. The camera next pans the table: the hands, fingers, wrists, watches, rings, June's black-red nails, the half-eaten food, the bread, the plates, the glasses, wine. Dinner sounds are amplified as if for radio, not film (the scrape of cutlery, the slop of drink, the strike of matches, the rub of soles, the over-miked conversation). A chrome light is suspended above the table, its light dimmer than the other lamps. Thus, faces are backlit, accenting shadowed close-ups and the smoke of cigarettes. The music, which fades, is jazz—Oscar Petersen, say, Stan Getz.

JUNE: *(Tilts her head toward me for a light for her cigarette. She keeps one eye on Kent, leans back, makes her smoking a production.)* Kent has given his heart to Trace. *(To include me)* Do you know Trace?

KENT: *(Also smoking, stubs his cigarette, then lifts, drains his glass.)* Most of us confine our assaults to dreams. My Junie works daytime too. Darling, you must be exhausted from your slaughters. The strain would accumulate, I'd think. How do you recover your strength?

JUNE: *(To me, but gazing at Kent)* Look at him. He's oxidized with love. *(To me, looking at me)* Do you know Trace? *(To Kent)* Would I be interested in your ruin? We're calling it slaughter now?

KENT: *(Lighting a new cigarette with a table candle, spills hot wax onto his wrist. He flinches, then intentionally burns himself again. June watches. Kent toasts June with a pull from his cigarette.)* You underrate yourself. You are not an unrealized assassin.

JUNE: *(Raises her glass)* God bless Trace. God bless her disposable self. Does she know?

KENT: *(To me, to involve me)* Our bed has been dead for years. *(To June)* If anyone wishes to think otherwise, that's their affair.

JUNE: Couldn't our poor sex life, at least, have been spared your grand ambitions? *(Then, rallying)* God bless this Trace. Does she know?

KENT: This dialogue *(He consults his watch)* took but seconds to speak, but rather a long part of my life to live. *(To June, directly)* Though it's not your fault. Dear June, you can't be blamed. Your need to kill is inscribed in every cell.

Kent sails into a lecture about genetics as the theory has applied to June. June squirms in her chair—a bored, naughty student with unmournfully large breasts. At one point, June accuses Kent of stealing their life script from the Swedish director Ingmar Bergman. ("Much of what we say," she says, "we stole from him.") June reaches over, empties the remainder of a wine bottle into Kent's glass, then gestures for Kent to drink. Kent stands, hoists the glass, drinks it off like an old Greek fisherman, flourishes the emptied glass, sits down. He stands back up with the glass, throws it. ("A nod to Albee," he says.)

Anna and I lacked such flair. We might have found port in such skills, but if we lacked exceptional performance, we didn't lack for a set: our final location Nebraska, the near exact center of the ontiguous United States. (Fold a map of the U.S. into fourths, hen open. The crosshairs are in Nebraska.)

Anna hated Omaha, said the city smelled. Omaha is (Coun-il Bluffs with its porn shops just across the once-unbridged Missouri) a city of railroads, insurance, national defense, cows, ilage, stockyards, slaughterhouses, and rendering plants where what's left of a cow is altered into wax, chicken food, bags of stuff or your grass.

I wasn't nuts about Omaha myself, but it was and is, each year, the site of the College Baseball World Series, and who can defame fully a city which hosts annually a baseball world series? The Omaha city fathers supported programs of *Peace through Strength,* baseball, and hale commerce. To put it otherwise: in Omaha people had jobs, religion, haircuts, steak, corn, trucks, plugged heart parts, dead cows, investment or term insurance, undressed women for the price of a drive across the Mighty Mo, the Air Force—nuclear protection and steady employment from Uncle Sam—and, once a year, a unifying community sport.

During the years we lived in Omaha, I escorted Anna to the College Baseball World Series, never missing a final game. I splurged for box seats a year in advance. But Anna hated Omaha, sang her refrain from the moment we motored across the city limits. She cranked down the car's front window, sucked a deep whiff of the life and death of cows on a southerly summer breeze: Jeezo. This city could ruin love."

We stayed in Omaha because Anna found work in a store called Queen's and because I snagged enough tuition assistance to finish grad school. Creighton University had a basketball reputation and mandatory class attendance—a time-honored Catholic tradi-ion. I attended class mornings, studied in the afternoons. Nights and weekends for the next two years, I worked in the Omaha stockyards where I met Spec Huff (a character Kent was to say my writer would've loved to have had at hand), my best Omaha al, and probably my wife's lover.

When my daughter and I left for Colorado, the last thing Anna barked on me was: *I also had Huff.* Spec had graduated (high honors) and was gone (I had the notion out West, where, I resumed, he was practicing physics). Spec fancied himself a prophet, though not one to warn the world so much against bombs as, more sensibly, against goons *with* bombs: Enlightened Science. He'd organized protests outside the gates of Headquarters Strategic Air Command, but the local media, in tight and uptight with the local military-industrial complex, had not bothered to notice.

What I recognize now—should have recognized before and repeated to myself like a parrot—is that if Anna and Spec, in fact, bewoggled each other breathless, then this was business between *them*, not business with *me*. How many years had it taken to chart this response? Meantime, the character Spec had not appeared, praised or damned, in any of my published stories. Nor, despite Kent's direct suggestions, was Spec present in any draft. I will tell you, though, some facts about Spec. Spec and I shared, for instance, twenty-seven months in the Omaha stockyards slopping shit.

Once, finishing late, and sitting in the locker room to rest, Spec and I stood aside for the passage of a winding row of Hasidic Jews. The rabbis, uncomfortably dressed for the heat of an Omaha August, changed from their shoes into rubber boots and switched to hard hats. The rabbis then rose as a group, headed out. Spec pinched my arm. We rose, covered, too, the frail bowl of our skulls with what seemed the frailer white molded plastic, and in that death house—safety on our heads, and in slogans above our lockers—tailed the Jews.

As a rule, cows at the yards were stunned by a shot from a pneumatic gun after which they were hung and bled, disemboweled, skinned. Kosher cows were strung up wide awake, their principal arteries opened perpendicularly to the axis of their necks, followed by inspection of their cooling hearts and lungs. This patterned slaughter was at the hand of only a handful of authorized Jews.

Spec and I were asked to leave. One of the rabbis, younger than the rest, stepped between Spec and me, rested his arms like a father about us. He craned toward the disciplined butchers. "For us this is prayer," he said, estimating us from a vantage of baggy eyes and brow. What should have been a young face seemed ancient, unbewildered, and—I couldn't decide—iron hearted? sad?

The death of a clear-headed cow a prayer? What message in that? That anything can be transformed and honored, converted to Truth? The rabbi, as I say, was young, but he made me feel younger. Spec and I turned from the wide-eyed dying and dead. We didn't bother the Jews again.

Though I was his peer, Spec treated me like a student. There were scientific things he thought I should know. For Spec, physics reigned supreme, and included, along with, say, the study of gravity or the curve of space, why chopping onions makes you cry. It was Spec's habit to educate me while we worked. His first lecture had been the physics which explained my pitchfork, an instrument Spec admired as evidence of applied science among early common people of divergent cultures. Spec preached that the pitchfork, in unadorned purity, had been present in civilization for as long as baskets and bread.

I asked Spec about black holes, because if he were going to teach me something, it might as well, I thought, be something I wanted to know. But Spec didn't answer my questions. He shut his eyes. Next night, Spec brought me a children's book, an oversize book with large pictures and print, and punchy sentences like *Well, what about black holes? Are they holes? Are they black? Let's look.* "Here," he said, thrusting the text at me. I took the book to understand black holes, but how to understand a force so transcendent even light is refused escape?

One night Spec hauled into the yards in his battered pickup, hammering the horn. He parked, then strode across the lot brandishing a golf club. Spec mounted the docks, set up with the club—a two-iron—took a healthy swing. We watched the perfect flight of an imaginary ball. Spec then announced he could drop a cow with a single blow. That broke the spell. We said, "You bet."

Spec dug in his pockets for chalk, scratched a formula on the cement—equations to transliterate his height, arm length and strength, club-head weight, speed, torques, the shift of arcs and planes. Spec stared at his math, then at us. But what he saw were not faces inspired by theory. One of the crew hefted Spec's club, pronounced it lighter than a good wood bat. The crew began to hoot. Spec raised his voice. His formula proved, he claimed, an actual ton of focused force. "One ton—do you hear?—of force."

We did the only thing we could: we collared a cow. Spec gazed around, then looked at me, then said, "Fine," then swung his club, loosening up. We rigged flooring the level of the heifer's head, which we then clamped between a couple of metal grates. We hobbled the cow, then lifted Spec to the makeshift floor.

We'd done a good job. The heifer couldn't move, and, confused, rolled her eyes. Someone said the cow was just looking for food; someone said, No, for God. The cow's display of bewilderment made my face go numb as if someone had popped a switch. I felt stupidly cruel but did nothing to halt what was now rolling full steam.

Spec looked at me. What did he expect? Would he have been satisfied with chalking his formula on the wall? Why had he brandished the club? Why had he brought it in? He'd raised the long iron above his head like a sword or wand—as if he were, what? a wizard? a saint? the Prince of Dung? Spec lined up his club on the heifer's ear. For the third and last time, he shot me a look. The crew, without me now, hooted louder. Spec settled on his heels, exhaled, drew back the club. In split seconds—head anchored, left arm rod straight, weight careening right to left— Spec had bent his club, fractured his wrist, and struck dead a Hereford the size of a Japanese truck.

The cow dropped, pulling with her the grates and the flooring. Spec, confoundingly athletic (few in that crowd would have thought of golf as a sport), leaped free of the heap, tumbling when he hit the slop off balance, cradling, protecting the wrist. He ended his roll on his feet, faced his work. Then a boss showed up. Except for Spec, we tried to scatter, but the boss shouted us back. We stood before him in a ragged row. Spec leaned against the docks. The boss swung from Spec to us, swore at us, spat, booted the cow, docked us an hour's pay, then stood while we— Spec didn't budge—hoisted the carcass to the blunt tines of a yellow forklift. We shambled back to our pens. The boss, from the wheel of the forklift, presided over this retreat, shifting his cigar, unlit in his mouth, and spitting. Spec outwaited the boss—who, in time, fired off with the cow and the forklift—then drove himself, manhandling his truck one handed, to the Medical Center at Creighton U.

That image of Spec—the club, the cow—is an image that sticks. I can be talking to anyone, anywhere, and I'll suddenly see the cow, hear the two-iron slamming home. The cow's eyes roll back. The film then rolls reverse and forward, reverse and forward, the cow's legs unfold and fold.

I felt some guilt about Spec's white-casted wrist, so I invited him to the house to watch Husker football on TV. I felt a sort of relief when Anna drew hearts and signed our names in blood red on Spec's cast. I kept fetching beer. We yelled for Nebraska to send the Sooners packing. We were happy. Spec pointed out that of a Saturday afternoon, Husker Stadium in Lincoln became the third largest city in the state. During the halftime on TV, Spec sobbed for having killed the cow. I pointed out, I thought sensibly, that the cow had been doomed. I reminded Spec of where we worked. "It's a slaughterhouse," I said. Spec refused the thought. In *cow* time and by *cow* logic, Spec argued, we had robbed a creature of days of food and breath. "We?" I remarked.

"You have to think about it like a cow," Spec said. When we'd drunk half a case, I conceded. Anna drove Spec's pickup to the 7-Eleven to get more beer. We kept the TV going but started a board game which ended when I challenged Anna on a move; she tossed the board, then left the house. I circled the floor on my knees, gathered the lettered squares.

The first time I was invited to Kent and June's, June tossed a Scrabble board, then her drink at Kent, then screeched off in her car. Kent and I watched her go, the convertible top lowered. Kent and I tramped back through the snow to the house, rubbing our arms. Inside, we poured drinks, cleaned up the game, searched for a lost square with the letter S. Lifting rugs, we treated the room in quadrants, scanned for a bump on the painted floor. We looked again. Buffaloed, we gave up. I said goodbye, drove home, thought of Spec—a name which started itself with S, stopped for beer, bought Stroh's, sped home, got drunk to Sinatra. Sinatra at the Sands. Was the mistake of my life, I wondered that night, blind drunk, not to have thought to have gambled in Las Vegas with Spec, not to have taken his mind to those tables?

Though when I think of Spec now—after sixteen years—I don't see him in casinos, I hear him preaching physics to half-filled halls in the intermountain West, up and down the knuckled spine of the Rockies. I've kept Spec thin, buzzed his hair, dressed him in chinos and ironed shirts, given his voice the sound of a bell: *There are no bystanders in a nuclear war or a bankrupt marriage.* I don't work to keep Spec in my mind: he's there. Before Spec. After Spec. Before I knew Spec I had a wife; after he left, I didn't. In between, he and I pitched a few tons of shit, stiffed a cow, studied the universe, maybe shared a lay, slugged beer. I've kept friends for less.

I finished at Creighton. Armed with a Master of Arts in English, I searched for a job teaching college. I couldn't find work, so I went back to the stockyards, nights. Daytime, I wrote short stories.

For her part, Anna advanced to a job with an insurance corporation. Part of the deal was Health and Life for herself, and, so covered, she investigated, famously stern is my bet, other people's claims. In a matter of weeks, she moved out of our house with Daniel. Daniel had turned two. Just learning to talk, he bumped around, bounced off furniture like a ball; in those days, if you spoke to Dan, he'd bite you.

Anna moved out with Dan, the living room, the bedroom, and most of the stuff from the kitchen. In her note she wrote: *I took some things. You're the one with the college degree. Alex is at school. Call you.* I fed and bathed Alexandra—her room and rituals intact. Alex had wanted to know what was happening. I had no idea what to say to a kid with a second-grade education; I kissed her till she pushed me away, then I covered her with extra blankets. In the living room, Anna had left the mirror tile she'd glued to one wall. The effect of this wall was to enlarge and distort the room. To save money when we moved in, Anna had widely spaced the tiles. Now ransacked but for one lamp and the mirrors, the room seemed large and overlit.

I stooped, raised, bent from side to side. All of me was there, but Anna's mirror wall demanded sequence and position. I gazed at the image: an ear gone there, fingers here, an eye. I stared at myself, then removed my clothes to look. In time, I turned to my bare windows. I switched off the light. Anyone could have seen me from the street.

Anna had cleared the room. Why did I stand naked in its barrenness, like the thief? When the telephone rang, I jumped, then bent to the receiver. I felt ready to confess. But to what? It was Anna who spoke: "You there?" Her voice sweetened: *It's not as if we can't talk.*

How do you account for the difference between what it was you wanted when you married and what you arrange for yourself to get? I stood in a museum in Philadelphia and stared at Kent's Trace. I'd not seen Anna in seven years. I counted it up, felt a slight panic, then took a good look at the art. It was not the type of art I was used to, but I felt drawn to the canvas painted to look like plywood hammered to the wall. It had fooled me until I got close. The painted plywood made me think of my dad: my father would have set the fake plywood's painted nails. As a kid, I was awed by my father setting nails, then masking the holes and sunk heads with blond putty.

From my father's nail set—its durable tip and crosshatched head—my attention transferred to Trace's legs. From a safe distance, I then returned my stare to *Red-Haired Woman*, the vinyl nude. Longer lasting than tin or bronze, this redhead would outlive me or Trace or anyone, but she'd do it without the pangs of doom, nostalgia, toil, alarm, fury, gesture, loss. I turned back to stare at Kent's Trace.

"You should meet her," Kent had said. "She's ferociously bright and able." For weeks, he wouldn't shut up. Finally, I asked if he'd mistaken confrontation and efficiency for intellect and knowledge, looks for beauty, pillage for response, and so on. But seeing Trace was, as Kent had suggested, a separate matter, another thing apart. From where I stood, Trace seemed in charge of herself and all about her: art and students, alive and dead.

"Have you seen her?" Kent asked, then looked past me to Trace.

"I found her." I pointed toward the class.

Kent checked his watch, checked Trace, who now was moving with her students. Kent said he'd found a meter. We turned, Kent and I, to *Wonder Bread*—six displays of sculpted sliced bread: carrara marble, 4 by 4½ inches. Six slices of poked, balled, folded—*mutilated*—bread. Everything you've ever done to Wonder Bread, or wanted to: in rock.

Kent said, what was this? I pointed at a banner. "Realism since 1960, Kent." I had become, in seeing Trace, an avowed and expert critic. I asked Kent what he thought Realism was, if *not* this.

Kent said he didn't know, but it was not stone bread. That a motorcycle leaned against a door could be no one's serious notion of a still life. I asked what he would prefer? stiff birds? a board of rotting fruit? "You want rabbits, Kent? Dead hares?"

"Yes," he said, then started for the restroom.

I felt condemned to a messier world than Kent's. "In the world of still," I shouted at his back, "there is no difference between a Buick and a grape." I felt half in love with Trace.

"Oh, of course there is," Kent said, without raising his voice or turning round. There was a bar of sweat where the back of Kent's shirt met his belt and slacks. Kent wore long-sleeved shirts year-round. Kent's hair, too, was damp. How far away had he parked the car? He'd found a meter all right—probably a meter with time, blocks away. Kent reached the stairs. I watched his wet head sink.

Kent was still gone when Trace joined me at the bread, one of her students following to ask should her reaction to the exhibition be technical or thematic. Trace nodded at the bread. I nodded at the bread. Trace waved the student off. "Make a choice," she said to the student, a pretty girl who could have used a bath. I wanted to offer the girl a good used crosshatch-headed nail set and unused bar soap: *tools for living*. The child beamed Trace a nasty look, then turned. Jealous as a daughter, she stamped off.

I looked back at Trace, a woman who surely would have understood the gift of setting the head of a nail in wood beneath the surface. At that moment, I wasn't certain I could teach college children again. Who can converse with beings who can't read without the honk of TV noise or rock? What sort of sounds would these children need to make love? Whatever happened to the music of night-long soaking rain? unmolested radio beams from Mars? wind in grass—natural sounds of truce and promise? I looked at Trace, convinced I could speak to no one but grown, educated, and employed adults. I started to say this when Kent shouted from the stairs.

Kent kissed Trace, then complained about the sculpted bread. I said Trace and I had met. I asked Kent would he approve of six diminutive nudes which, like the glassed-in bread, had been variously offended and displayed? I turned to the shabby leather valise, which we found to be constructed—including its rubbed brass corners—of high-fired ceramic clay.

"Wonderful," said Trace.

On the wall were canvases of pickups and semis: painted portraits so precise they looked like photos. One of the pickups could have passed for a replica of Spec's, the exact rust and dents. Part of me wanted to see old Spec in the painting too, slouched, say, in the background against the barn's wood sides or swinging an iron. Then a picture of Anna and Spec unclothed on a bed flashed as on a screen. I shook the image off. I looked at Trace and Kent. Then, as will happen, I saw the cow. I drove the heifer from my mind, looked again at Trace. For an instant, I saw Trace as June: a trick of mind and light. The phenomenon, though short-lived, seemed true, like a religious vision.

Kent's wife, June, applies mascara perfectly. Large women are careful that way, and sad. And June, too, in the past twelve months, has deserved attention, even care. I've suggested this to Kent, have mentioned professional help. "Yes, of course you're right," he says. He nods his head. "You're right."

Kent moved from his house into a condo, and June began to visit me. "What am I supposed to do?" she'd ask. I'd return her look, then mix us drinks. She'd claim the couch, sink in, weep. She seemed certain that for the remainder of her life no one would ever follow her, trail her on a street. Inverse paranoia. She'd weep, then threaten suicide. Finally, I said, "Well, June, it's a choice."

Saturday, the following week (Alex, by chance, spending the night with friends), June stopped by. Returning from the kitchen with fourth-round drinks, I interrupted June. She was stuffing her brassiere into her purse. She leaned back: spread her blouse, dimmed the lamp, reached up for her drink. She smelled of lanolin and rain.

I sat across the room.

What I wanted were the breasts; what there also was, was June. I asked June to dress. She tipped her drink into her lap. I stood to help, but June waved me off. I retook my seat, and we both sat, host and guest, while a good wool skirt absorbed Scotch. June's skirt so drew our attention that it took on a presence we both embraced. June paid attention to the skirt, plunked ice back into her glass. I stayed on my side of the room, watched her do it.

In time, she stood, a final, dazed, halfhearted display—a wan band of fat folding at her hips—then stepped, transporting the remainder of her drink, to the bathroom in the hall. I watched June step away. Staring at her clothed back, I calculated the swing of the bare front.

June disappeared from the hall to the bathroom; as she pivoted, I caught a last glimpse. June saw I had; she froze for the merest second, shoulders hunched, then beamed me the sweetest smile. I'd finished my drink when June emerged. She came to me; we held. "My chest is my best thing," she said. "Your chest is wonderful," I said. June didn't stop her visits, but she managed to stay dressed.

Kent, like June, is in his forties. As such stories go, he and Trace's husband, Ray, were fraternity brothers as undergraduates in Ohio, where June was the Sweetheart of Sigma Chi and Kent the Army ROTC detachment cadet commander, which was as much a reason as any why they wed and then rode out an additional twenty-five years. That, and the glue of anyone's marriage: houses and children and dogs. Oriental rugs. The signed prints you buy one summer—the children still small—in Duluth. Applewood being burned. Snow. Tulips. A great-aunt's crystal swan. Shingles shedding rain. The scent of oyster stew.

Kent claims he didn't know Trace at college, that he met her the day she married Ray. At Case Western in Ohio, Kent was a student who carefully read writing texts and since has written three: *Freshman Composition I, II,* and *III.* He's sold these books, to his embarrassment, he claims, but also collects, each year, the royalties and is working on a fourth, *Freshman Composition IV.* He invests the money in his own hot-air balloon, which, tethered, outrises a seven-story house. "In the air," he says, "she swims."

I tell Kent the whole thing strikes me as a bother. I wave at the propane tanks; the flame; the thick-caned graceless basket. "And goddamned dangerous," I say. I mention power lines and trees. "Rocks, Kent. Water. *The necessity to land.*"

If Kent is near enough to the basket, he'll rub the cane. "In the air," he says, "she swims." Kent seems armored beyond any of my friends, protected by dull-witted but attentive angels. It makes you not want to think.

An accredited English scholar—quite apart from the freshman texts—Kent calls himself a hack. He'll publicly threaten retirement and the penning of a novel, then laugh. "Stop it," I say. "What you live is your life. Not all problems can be solved by writing fiction."

"That's just not so," he says.

"Like hell it's not," I say.

Kent knows this at least as well as I, but after a life of achievement, he will become, at times, boozily contrite for his central professional coup: a critic's orderly arrangement of myth. *The tidy myth dictionary,* he says. *The hard cover a student will buy.*

"Does buy," I correct. "Stop apologizing, Kent."

"You," says Kent. "You shake the moon."

What do you do with a man like Kent? You drive him home. You can do that. You put him in his bed.

For a hundred and eighty bucks, Kent will bear two customers aloft. He sails, bargaining with wind. "Up there," he says, "you don't fight the wind. You're it." He sails in full or veiled sun. He serves champagne.

On the evening of the day we met, Trace turned from the front seat of the car, "Stephen, you do everything so quickly." In the dark, I looked at the back of Kent—his hands in charge of the moving car—then stared at Trace. Later that first night—Kent at the bar for drinks—Trace asked if Kent would do coke. I said I didn't know. Trace opened her purse, then stopped, "I see." Whether Trace had cocaine in her purse, I don't know. She may have been thinking of testing me, or of testing Kent, or not.

My first letter to Trace was short. I wanted to ask whether she told her husband when she had other men. I asked instead, "Will you marry Kent?"

Kent is not, by nature, smug. But I wearied of his talk of Trace. I wearied of his luck, his trust: a ballooner's simple faith in the properties of air. I wanted Trace. But you knew that, as well as you know that Kent is no cartoon. I blamed him for his luck. I blamed him for June's fat. You find ways.

"Will you marry Kent?" I asked.

"I may marry Kent," Trace said.

Trace and I never went to bed. I wrote to her. She wrote to me, and she would visit Kent. Once, in my and Kent's town, we met for lunch. "What did you say to Kent?"

"I told him I'd be with you," said Trace. "I told him I was going to lunch."

She'd brought summer berries from her parents' farm and had saved a pint for me. I pictured her on the plane, jars of berries in her lap. *You have no decent fruit in Colorado. Here, I've brought you fruit.* That night she and Kent returned to Pennsylvania. I drank and wrote letters. Here is one I sent:

Fruit is available in my state. Aridity and altitude are easy marks for long-haul truckers, hiked costs. Though it's dusk, you can see the sun for the first time in three days. You should know that, two blocks from where we lunched, a "mini-tornado" carried away part of the roof of a discount dental clinic. But what is a "mini-tornado"? For the dental clinic—cut-rate or not—wasn't it A TORNADO?

———————

I wrote more letters. Weeks later she answered back—a letter about her husband:

Raymond has Guillain-Barré syndrome—the swine flu virus some people got two years ago following their flu shots. Raymond has lost all motor ability. Thursday I took him home from the hospital again. Someday, if you ask, I will speak to you of that— the *quiet*. R. has not taught since the end of this spring term. He spent twenty-four days in a hospital bed and has been back in again. He'd never been in a hospital before. I've moved back into the house. I miss Kent. I miss you. The woman you choose is destined for some pain, for you do dole out the latter whenever you see fit. Women are accused of being contrived, but you—you do your share. I wish you were here now. Take care of Kent, take care of you. Please tell me what is real.

"Tell you what is real?" I wrote. Then:
Charlie Chaplin once entered a Charlie Chaplin look-alike competition. Charlie came in third. How would I know what's real?

I suppose I could have said that Trace and I went to bed and, with that step, stepped into the other's life forever—that we discovered realms. But we didn't go to bed; we wrote. Trace divorced Ray. She hadn't loved him when he was well. And Kent divorced June, with the finality of that act seeming to be of help to her. *The finality of acts.* The benignity, the imperative of rites: champagne in flight; darker wine in church; food offered as gift, as sacrament. *Flesh.*

Trace called to say she and Kent had picked a date. I asked about Ray. She said he was still confined to bed. "His mother's back," she said. "I can't be ungrateful to her for that."

So Trace arrived in the fall in Colorado, ready to marry Kent. The night she arrived was her birthday and was the eve of mine, so the three of us met for dinner—Kent's idea—a combination *fête*. Kent and Trace were late, so I waited at the bar. When they walked in, Trace handed me, for my birthday, a loaf of fresh-baked bread she had carted on board the plane from Pennsylvania.

You have no decent bread in Colorado. I didn't choose to share the bread. At dinner, I tightened the waxy bag, laid it at my feet.

After dinner, we moved outside the restaurant with drinks and sat, in coats, around a fire a waiter had replenished and banked: no place, Trace said, to speak of domes or marble. The courtyard was stone and dirt and had fire pits with facing benches. There was a rail fence. Trace pointed to the restaurant behind. "Adobe is mud," she said. "Yes," said Kent. They turned to me. I nodded my head: *agreed*. We were drunk in the dark. We were, stubbornly, the three of us, bareheaded. The ground at our feet was cold. The busboys had begun to clear inside, the waiters to compute their tips. The night seemed vast; the city glittered. The city reminded me of hospital stainless steel, flashing back directed light. I leaned back from the fire, breathed in; the air smelled of scorched metal.

A waiter first brought out wood, then another round of drinks. He looked outward from the bluff which rose above the roads, the complex luminescence: a ballooner's restaurant, said Kent. "Last call," the waiter replied, then handed us our drinks. "My round," I said, standing, holding to the night, rooting for my wallet. The waiter grinned, offered back no change. You could almost see his breath. You could see his teeth.

When I sat, I reached to touch my bread, its wrapping as warm as the cloth of my pants. In the morning, I would eat the bread, and the morning after that. I sat and drank. My hands had the feel for me of having encircled iron rails or the cold runners of a sled. I thought of the dead steel blades of skates and that one winter before I was born I'd had a sister who had died on New Year's Day because she'd chewed a Christmas ornament made of glass. Did my baby sister, absent now forty years, think she'd bitten into a plum? "My grandfather was a light heavyweight," I said. "His name was Arthur Mann. He whipped the light heavyweight champion of the world."

Kid Dixie had barnstormed through Butte, Montana, on the train, set up a ring, offered to take on comers—winner-take-all—nontitle. It was 1936. My grandfather removed his shirt, put out his hands for gloves. He stepped through the ropes in his work shoes. It was a rough affair. The champ wasn't having his way and panicked. My grandfather could fight and had no intention of lying down. He crowded the champ, bore in, whaled on the champion's ribs. Then, in the fourth round, his own right eye punched shut, Arthur knocked Kid Dixie on his can: a right—all instinct—from his blind right side to the champion's jaw. The punch traveled less than a foot.

The crowd went nuts. One-eyed, my grandfather Arthur took the cash, climbed from the ring, walked home with his son, my father. How many chances like that does a father have? Would Arthur have tried, even in his dreams, to live another life?

And me? I'd separated my kids—brother and sister—and lived a professional life which had long rested, not on a win-or-lose fight, but on the writing of an unread book. Would my son's son remember me? What stories could he tell? I began to ask myself some questions: could I truly say I wanted my friend's balloon? Let's say, I said to myself, Kent's balloon was actually mine. Was it in me to trust a means of travel fueled by mere heated air? And how to calculate this mistrust? a strength? a flaw? I couldn't answer my own questions, so I closed my eyes. I looked for Spec's cow, but didn't see her. What I saw was a diagram of a black hole, a schematic, from Spec's book of the unseeable death of stars.

"Of da world?" Kent asked.

I turned to Kent, opened my eyes.

"Of da world?" he said.

Kent's face in focus, I drew breath.

Kent flailed a fist in the dark. "Your grandfather," he said.

I thought about that—my grandfather had licked the light heavyweight boxing champion of the world—yes, that was something. My father had told me the story. If the story wasn't true, I thought, it should be. I raised my glass toward Kent. "Of da world," I said. Kent stuck out his glass, clinked mine. But before he drank, he ducked, shot another almost savage punch toward his ghost opponent.

I thought about my grandfather again—Kid Dixie knocked bowlegged to his back on the canvas. For four rounds in 1936— the third round shaved thirty seconds, Dixie's manager as panicked as his champ—in a broken country, *winner-take-all*, two men had worked to earn their livings. It seemed impossible in a night so vast not to crave such an even chance at victory or defeat. No split decision.

I poked my hands at the fire.

Trace stared and stared at stars: red giants and white dwarfs.

"Just when you need your father's father," I said, "he's been dead for twenty years. When I die," I asked, "who will be left to love him?"

Kent tossed what was left of the wood into the fire, which we circled and which blazed, but we still all huddled closer, cradling our drinks. Fire and ice. And wind, baked stone. Kent turned, then stood to see if there were more wood piled about. "The restaurant looks closed," he said.

I unwrapped my bread, tore off chunks. We chewed the bread, and drank. I kissed Kent and Trace, then sat back down, leaned forward. What I wanted to feel was seemliness and love, but what I felt was scalded by the dry wood's high flame.

On the highway below, the traffic was mostly truckers—mirror constellations, untimed, unplanned—the lapses in between rich, small black holes.

You let yourself look up, but what stars watch is not your life.

"Of course they don't. You watch them," says Trace.

You stare at Trace. Have you been speaking aloud?

You tip your head. All you see is sky: *Andromeda. Centaurus. Giant Orion, the Hunter Taurus. Red-Haired Nudes. Glimmering, Velvet Chairs.* By means of dead or living light, you map the path of worlds: bright soot. And time.

The
Art
of
Fiction

Writing Assignments. (Choose one)

1. Take in a museum series of a woman's face: six photos. In each enlarged black-and-white, the woman's face (a slip away from plainness) lures, broaches, transfixes, pricks. Beneath each view of the face, in this sequence, in the artist's pencil cursive: *Mother, Father, Sex, God, Death, Self.* And to introduce the photos: *The camera trained on Lisa was controlled by her. I provided the six words in sealed envelopes. In a darkened room, Lisa confronted, six times, a word. At the moment Lisa possessed the image or memory by which she most embraced each faced word, she triggered the shutter:*

EXERCISE: Consider the effect of such an experiment for you, then compose six stories: *Mother, Father, Sex, God, Death, Self.*
EXTRA CREDIT: Snap/Develop the photos. Cope.
HELPFUL HINT: Memory is Imagination.
PROBLEM: Memory is Imagination.

2. Flex critically. Pen an essay embracing the vast terrain of story. Consider, as a minimum, who you or we are—any of us—to suppose to slip the summons of time, failure, tribe, success, panic, decent want, insanity, death, fashion, entitlement, lucidity, quiddity, impotence, license, humility, blood, shame, arrival, unsettled grief, vision, terror, perfidy, loss, fortune, pity, art, error, heaven, truth—*mutinous* truth, sympathy, surrender, avoidance, damage, history, sperm, agency, tallying competition, self-pitying self-importance, glamour, turbulence, egg, chaos, inaction, imploration, tyranny, defiance, mask, horror, intention, invention, rites, discovery, recovery, sweet order, troth, ire, murk, pox, sorrow, clemency, inoculation, viscissitude, love? Be sure to include a thesis statement.

3. Or, hell, write a story about your dog:
a. Your dead dog
b. When your father came home, Naps was under the tire (the car still in neutral, brakes off).
c. Because, even with your father's help, you couldn't push the dead car up the incline off Naps, so your father flagged down a neighbor.
d. Because when the neighbor nudged his gas to nudge your father's car off Naps, his bumper rode up over your father's, locked, doubled the car's rear weight.
e. Because you had planned to recharge the battery by revving the car (by driving it out past the *Tastee-Freez*, then back).
f. Because you had a buck in your pants for gas.
g. THE DOG YOU CRUSHED WITH YOUR FATHER'S CAR.
h. Because you planned to coast the car down the incline of your street (switching the key, popping the clutch) to start it.
i. Because as the battery bled, you twisted up the volume (heavy treble, light bass).

j. Buddy Holly, Richie Valens, The Big Bopper *(Oh, Baby, you KNOW what I like!).*

k. Because, long tuned to the yowl of the faulty starter, what reason had Naps to scramble?

l. The car (your father's, not your neighbor's): a 1949 green Hudson Hornet.

m. White whitewalls as wide as your palm.

n. As wide and white as your palm.

o.

Weather

My father, who like his father before him had worked gold claims in Alaska, had lost his trust in machines in the cold. Stranded once, my father had forfeited parts of fingers and toes and sported a crater on his nose where the metal frame of his eyeglasses had welded to flesh and torn a hole when he'd pulled to remove them.

Warned of storm, my father, Harry, wouldn't have budged from home in a car or a plane—*a bulldozer, snowplow*—nothing engined. During temperatures below twenty below, he refused, even, to use phones. As for winter machines, Harry, in particular, questioned snowmobiles—no windshield, no roof, no heater, no way to belt in, *no heater.* The first time he saw a snowmobile I was with him. We had seen them of course on TV—muscular ads for black Ski-Doos—then we saw two flying through our neighbor's hilly, cleared fields, swerving to miss the fences, circling to vault the ditch. *Out-of-bounds caper,* my father put it. We'd heard the machines and stepped to the porch. The temperature was not above zero. My father occupied his porch, which by some quirk of angle and position the wind kept swept of snow, and pulsed the shut hinge of his jaw. The pink crater on his nose discolored.

Shadowed by the slant and pour of sun, the Ski-Doo tracks, like topographer's marks, mapped the hills. Harry raised his chin: "Looks like dirt on soap." Seeing us, the black bugs buzzed off. You could hear the drivers whooping.

The smarter Indians in the North—*real* Indians—Harry instructed that night at dinner, wouldn't trade in their dogs or their sleds for powered mowers. "That's what they are," Harry said, "doctored mowers." From the table, he pointed through the dining room wall towards the drivers. But it was night now, and the drivers and their machines were gone, hours gone. Harry agreed with himself: "*Clowns.*"

This was the winter of my final year of high school. Eighteen, I'd begun working underground weekends and holidays at the mines and had registered with the Selective Service. I began to explain to my father that we didn't live in the Yukon, that *normal* people on weekends played, and, what was more, had the perfect right to. Harry replied that, Christ, he knew, Goddamnit, that we didn't live in the Yukon, but that these sort of fads had a way of working north and confusing the natives. And what did I mean by normal? "Normal? You want normal? Innocence is fooled. That's normal. We'll do 'em in yet," he said. "Just like we did Chief Joseph."

The last thing I wanted was my father full steam on the long-gone, noble Nez Perce, so I shot my brothers looks. I opened and closed my mouth for them to see I was biting on words. Among Harry's principal topics besides Technology versus Weather was The Indian, and it looked as though his two main groups—the Eskimo and Nez Perce—were rising like fish, twisting for lures. But if we were careful we could limit the night to one tribe, was my hope.

Weather   43

At some point, after I'd left Montana—for college in Utah, then Vietnam—it came to me that among the reasons my father esteemed Eskimos was because he believed they'd stayed where they belonged. *Eskimos still fish the North,* I'd heard him time and again say. *You don't find them in Seattle.* I discovered, too, that the Nez Perce, although a sizable tribe, had managed, within years of defeat and containment, to assimilate into the general population.

Back at the dinner table, Harry shook his head. "You don't see it, do you?" Harry made a point to survey the table, but he was talking to me. My brother, Robert, pointed a finger at me, then stood with his plate. *You,* he mouthed.

"Since when?" Harry said. "*Sit.* Stay tuned." Though my brothers were only two and three years younger than I, my father treated them as children. "You, too," he said to Harold, Jr., the youngest.

My mother stood to clear the table. My father smiled at her, turned back to me. He wanted to talk, he said, about The North and Eskimo dogs, which was, in truth, about the Lower 48 and Ski-Doos. "You get in a bind up there without your dogs, what are you going to do, eat your engine?" Then: "You're my oldest," my father said to me, "you're the oldest." Robert was beaming me toxic looks. Even Junior turned coat, gave me a look like he was gagging, then pretended he was really throwing up. My mother called from the kitchen. I waited for Harry to stop Junior like he'd stopped Robert, but he focused on me.

"You have to know in this world what's what." What, at that moment, in this world Harold Arthur Mann, my father, knew was he detested snowmobiles—the whine of their sissy motors, the idea of their weekend use, the mere thought of their frolicking owners. He carried on about the owners then moved to the million-dollar rock band who in naming themselves had trivialized his Eskimos' sweet accurate poetry for cold: Three Dog Night—*Serious business in the North,* he said, *not some hippies pimping songs. Dope and songs won't keep you warm. A goddamned song won't save you.*

For my father, there was little in the world as permanent or deadly as people's folly, and he worried for his sons. In the sixties when my brothers and I were still at home and in school, Harry would lower his *Life* or *Look* to reaffirm his views on dope and songs—and this: that girls' beads were for girls, and that growing long hair was what it was—growing hair—and for an amazing and increasing number of male losers, their sole and chief goal, and probably life's achievement.

Harry had read somewhere about hippies sleeping naked in piles and said that was no fantasy of his. He said they had whole Broadway shows, for Christssake, in New York, with naked actors. *That where you want to find your bride,* he'd ask when our mother wasn't about, *bare assed on some stage, in a pile? You going to pull from the top of the pile? The bottom? A woman with dust on her ass? You ask me, theaters like that would be dusty. Sad assed and dusty. If you don't know about this, then I'll tell you. Because you should know.*

Harry showed me a *Life* feature about Charlie Parker and Dizzy Gillespie and Miles Davis. My father didn't listen to jazz, and probably hadn't read the article he was explaining. What he said was that drugs were for black musicians. He said, "Why do you think they call this bird, Bird—*Yard*bird? Why do you think they call this one 'Dizzy'?" Harry fingered on the page a young Gillespie.

"Dizzy's real name is John," I said, because I knew, and because at school I had heard recordings. I studied the photo. Dizzy had on some sort of African cap and plastic-rimmed glasses, which, I almost said, wouldn't freeze to his nose.

"And there's this other one here called Miles." Harry turned the page. "See," he said, "*Miles.*" Worship in his eyes, a young Miles Davis was gazing at Dizzy. "Drugs will make you feel like an old car," Harry said. "You understand what I'm trying to tell you? There's a drug shift to whites, you follow? To the palookas with the hair and the beads and the bandannas. You know who I mean, you know what I mean, and you watch it. You watch for your brothers, too. You're the oldest."

"I'm growing hair," Junior said, back from the kitchen, slouching against the door frame. "I'm going to worship Buddha. I'll probably need drugs. That stuff Apaches can make from cactus."

But Harry was talking to me about drugs and blacks and white palookas. He told me to watch it, too, with booze. His father, Arthur, had died an alcoholic. "Booze troubles jump through a son to a son, so you watch it. I love you." Harry raised a finger to my face, then included Robert and Junior with a grand sweep of his arms. "You are my sons," he announced. "You are all my sons, and I love you."

If worry is proof of love, then Harry, our father, loved us. He taught us all, early, to drive, then worried about wrecks—he brooded. He worried about VD and gave us the lectures he'd heard in the Army, or the lectures he'd heard when he'd tried to join up. Harry'd been refused enlistment because of a damaged eye, but had received the warnings he passed on whole to us— all the warnings that didn't save careful Americans at Anzio or Okinawa or wherever it was my father was saved from.

My father, Harry, worried about communists, bombs and defective condoms, deep water, the aggressive unexaggerated shadow of iron lungs, untrained horses, economy, frostbite, hard women, storm—any error we could commit that would last us. And now, just this side of forty, still Harry's oldest and, among his sons, the longest beneficiary of his advice, I'd driven my car—a *machine*—into storm (on the radio news, a fifty-nine-car pileup on I-70 near Denver) to see another man's wife.

The weather that had been predicted was belting Colorado. And here, along the spine of the Rockies' front range, skirting the plains, nothing curbed the wind, and chill factors were flirting with sixty below—too cold, by far, for phones. You could tell that drifts, before long, would close roads, cover stalled cars, kill cattle. *Real cold doesn't reduce heat and light,* was a theory of my father's. *It outmuscles it,* Harry said. *Crushes.*

In storm that could kill, I was driving miles to see a woman who belonged to a friend—double or triple sins I could not have confessed to Harry. I could not have said, "Yes, Andrew and I were friends, but Suzanne and I became better ones." Or, "Look, you tend to fall in love with the people you know." Or, "This has nothing to do with Andrew; it has to do with Suzanne and me." I couldn't even have said, more simply, "I think I'm in love. It's possible we're in love." Harry responded to an older, more alert god for whom confession brought consequence as often as absolution. I didn't intend to put myself into such a position with my father by confessing, though I could hear him nonetheless: *You* drove into weather for what? A piece of tail? You don't risk your life for a woman you love. You stay alive for her, that's what. Are you confused, because you seem confused? Who is she? Is she married? Is that it? Is that what this is? Do you love her? Then: What color is she? Is she colored?

Scaling Ice

Mush yourself to the North or South Pole, either icecap. Chip from a glacier for your drink. (You have brought, certainly, a tumbler?) Add gin, room-temperature tonic. The air escaping the cleaving ice is unpolluted. Give pause and ear to the whisper—vaunted—of the ages: a gassy tale ten thousand years told. *Inhale.* You could ask a question now, but what? Is what you feel in this unadministered place a renunciation of your ambitions? It may be you must admit to no confusion here on this lidded retina of the planet, to no sound of wind-chattered flowers, grass. Why is it you feel no sacrifice, profundum, gain, loss? Will you find it simpler mushing in than out (as to and from a woman)?

Or is this about blunt waiting: the shift, in the cold, from one foot to the other, grubbing for lore, instruction? What is it you have for exchange: fur, soy, clams, fruit? a strong dog's lung? some other untried church?

Would
You
Feel
Better?

_____

Two weeks ago from Utah, Andrew, Suzanne's husband, on the phone: *You son of a bitch, I know about you. Don't think I don't.* And, yesterday: her. Suzanne wanted this, her call, to be final. *Let's settle this on the phone.* Suzanne said she wanted to put Andrew on the bedroom extension. *Anything you have to say to me now he should hear.*

"I've told Andrew if he bothers you or tries to hurt you in any way that I'd leave. That I'd go with you. I've told him."

"Then go with me."

"Don't joke."

"I've missed you."

"I'm not leaving Andrew, Stephen."

"I miss you."

"I thought I was more certain."

"You told Andrew about us, because you're weren't certain? And after you told him, you were certain? You had need of a bad conscience, so you trotted one out? Without talking to me, you told him?"

"Anything you have to say to me now my husband should hear. My husband should hear it."

"I have plenty to say he should hear."

Suzanne said we should get things settled.

"Sometimes, Suzanne, I don't think of you for hours and it's perfect, it's lovely. I love you."

"Do you know what he said when I told him? He said, 'If you were going to leave—*if you meant to leave*—why didn't you tell me before I hung all this paper?' Andrew wallpapered the house, Stephen. I don't mean he had it done—I mean he did it."

"If you want out, OK, but spare me the hubby stories." I told Suzanne there were bones in my head I felt shifting.

"Then sit down."

"I am sitting."

"You should sit." Then: "I'll not be a monument to celebrate the innocence of your faith in love."

"Wow. You rehearse that? I'm feeling confused, Suzanne. I feel confused."

"You seemed pretty unconfused about what we were doing. In your heart, Stephen, you're a vacation lover. You know what you want, admit it. You were clear about it, and your timing was not always perfect. Your timing was often unkind."

"Tell Andrew you're coming to see me. No, put him on, I'll tell him."

"You don't mean this, Stephen, so stop. It's not what you want. Andrew, for all his faults, does know me. He knows me."

"Is this about money, Suzanne? Because if this is about money."

"How would you like to have to ask me for money for a haircut or something? My money's all tied up with Andrew. Whatever money Andrew and I have made apart, we've multiplied together.

I paid for my own plane fares when I came to you. That was important to me. It was important to you, too, if you'd admit it. I can't come to you broke and I can't come to you with money. I can't come."

"Don't tell me this on a phone."

"You think I wouldn't tell you this to your face? You think I couldn't tell you in person?"

"Then do it," I said. "Tomorrow. Do it then."

It took as long for me to drive from my house to the Denver airport as it took for Suzanne to fly in, and, as I would point out, there was decent liquor served on all flights. It was a joke we had about Utah.

"Tomorrow, Suzanne. How bad could it be? An hour in the air. Two drinks."

"There's a storm building. A major winter storm. It's on all the news."

"An historic storm," I said. "*A killer.*"

"Say whatever you want, but it's predicted."

"The Storm of the Century."

"I gave what I wanted, Stephen. Tell the truth, you know that. You want everything."

"I love you."

I dialed back.

"Why'd you tell Andrew before me?"

"You'll wake up tomorrow."

"I'll wake up all right, and I'll be at the airport. I have something Andrew should hear. Put him on."

"Forget I said that. I shouldn't have said that. I'm sorry I said it. Don't dial back again, please. I don't want to take the phone off the hook. I don't want to have to. Stop."

"Whose vacation was it when you were with me and away from your home? I was home, you were traveling. You're the traveler, Suze. If it's any of my business, how much of all this did you know when we started?"

"It's your business or not. Anyway, I don't know. So."

Near midnight, I phoned Suzanne. I asked if she thought I could be killed calling from a phone in a tub.

"You're in the bathtub now? How much water?"

I detected a tingling in the fingertips of the hand holding the phone above the filled tub, a distant pulse up my arm. I asked to speak to Andrew.

"Andrew's not here."

"It's you I want to talk to anyway. He's gone?"

"I've heard of people in tubs being killed talking on phones, but during electrical storms, summer storms. It's snowing there, right?" Then: "You might as well know he packed when I told him. He wasn't here when I said I was going to put him on the phone. I just said so, but he'll be home."

"You sound certain. I'll say that."

"Grief about lost pleasure and fear of losing pleasure come to the same. You clambered after us so much it made me afraid. What can you enjoy if you fear in your enjoying you'll lose it?"

I said I believed that together we'd found something worth guarding.

"Things get lost that are guarded. Locked houses get robbed, Stephen. Guarded houses give burglars desire as well as reason."

"*Burglars with desire and reason?* Good Lord, do you hear us?"

"Last week, in my neighborhood, a burglar washed a stack of dirty dishes then took a shower before he emptied the house of all of its electronics and jewels. He washed the dishes, mopped the kitchen floor, plus he scrubbed the shower after he'd used it. Then he took everything. Do you believe it?"

"What are you saying?"

"Andrew and I have a life. We have years and things. We can refer to a past. What you and I had were vacations. How would you prefer I put it, Stephen? Would you feel better if I said Andrew bought new patio furniture and that I like it? Would that make you feel better?" she asked, then hung up.

Bliss

You rise to light, drumming rain. These dawns you run alone, trying new routes, and it's bliss.

You slow as you come upon a woman in her nightclothes. She faces away, standing in her yard, crying. You think at first for birds, for she holds birdseed in her hands, thrusting at the world like a statue or saint. But her sounds are unbirdy. Is it she cries out, not to birds at all, but in pain? An appeal to bone-wet trees? sky? The air above the yard is the color of unoxidized steel.

A man steps to the porch to face you and the road. He smokes, gray suited, deaf to the woman, blind to you. He raises a hand to scratch at his nicked cheek (the blood is beaded, you are certain, and congealed).

Bagged grass forms dams at the curb.

You see these things—the man, the woman, the roofed porch, the curb flush, the fleeced lawn, the man's shaved cheek, the sad absence of birds—with the access, easy struggle, and simultaneity of dream.

The woman in her nightclothes keens. Her bare heels are cracked, stuccoed with grass. The grass seems unnaturally green.

A German car has been backed from the garage and left running. The man on the porch tilts his head toward the sound of the engine, then jars ash from his cigarette, as though the ash had prevented him from fitly judging the hum.

There's no escape for you. There is: the man's shut face, the woman's back, the cigarette, the rain-webbed grass, the lead light, sky. The wail, the cupped seed, the creased heels, the tuned snarl of an expensive foreign car. The unceasing sneak of stars. Your own bleak breath. Your own void breath in the cold. You stand, half dressed in the street, ashiver, sweating.

The woman will stalk you all the day. Will she peck the seed in her palms? flaunt wings? soar? In the hard dark light, unseen birds now flap wet black wings, chirr. You strain and strain to hear and think of water-slick, cold stone; slunk tides; a woman's knobbed spine; sand; the silvered bellies of fish, beached, gilling, desperately, rain.

Barrie Hooper's Dead

Barrie Hooper's dead.

I sit in *Poor Richard's* restaurant and used book store—*Poo Richard's Read & Feed*—which has just reopened after months repair. Someone tried to burn the place, setting three spaced, in ternal fires.

Mrs. Hooper has returned letters I'd sent her daughter. But th mother has marked those private words with hers: notes to her self? to me? She's made a Xerox of this work. I stack what are no *our* letters—Barrie's, Mrs. Hooper's, mine—then order Mexica beer, then wait.

Mrs. Hooper has written.

The survival of the race depends on love—you're correct. It's a natural heat, but you're living several degrees below it. I don't like you. Not at all.

I hail the stir of five new women who pause to survey. They elect a wall table. These women storm us (who have staked our claims) with the noise of life. They pretend to be abroad. French house wine—*table wine*—is what they order. That, and feta cheese, bread, tomatoes, Greek olives. One of the women, the one gumming cigarettes and reading Margaret Drabble, inquires as to whether the olives will come unpitted, sighs, then returns to her book. A page or two in, she pronounces Drabble *fit*, situates the book, open paged and facedown, on the table.

The women light one another's cigarettes, pour one another's wine, and stretching to the shelves beside them, collect and pass arty greeting cards the restaurant stocks and sells. I eye their ears and throats and breasts, the stiff flutter of their wrists.

One of the women runs her fingers through her hair, which she's probably cropped herself. She thinks she portrays something—a traitor to the French Resistance? Joan of Arc? a de-frocked Swiss nun? The thin woman registers my gawk, projects me back, her hand working the hair.

The greeting cards recircle the table. The women argue names of artists: Rothko, O'Keeffe, Matisse. "I missed that?" the tall one asks. She checks the back of one of the cards, slaps herself in the head: "I missed it."

"You missed it," avers the leader, the one with the book and the largest earring.

Which swings against her neck.

They eat and drink, but, in time, the women rise, as if on cue, to leave. Why should women who don't want men dishearten or rile me? My father, were he living and sitting with me, certainly would have advised me to let the women be, but never would he have pretended to have understood. *Two of them are beauties. See.*

I work to project my father's feelings across the room, but the women don't peep back. A waiter clears their table, returns Drabble to the shelves, which, after the fire and the repair, the customers have helped restock with their own old paperbacks and texts.

I check the room for former or present students.

In this restaurant, you see kids passing high-priced grass wh
discussing the wholesomeness of water-processed decaffeinat
coffee. In the stories these students write for class, their hero
sooner or later, fight for rain and wind and light, love wha
and Buddy Holly, whom they can have seen only, if at all,
tape. More depressing than cheering, I'm seeing, again, the wor
of my own passed youth: SPACESHIP EARTH. FARMS NOT ARMS. LO
ME DO.

Without my asking, a waitress brings a second Corona. I pun
the lime wedge down the bottle neck, then pour about half
glass. The waitress hangs around, fiddles with the empty bott
We both reach to finish pouring the second bottle into the gla
She looks me straight in the eye. "You starved?"

The taped music—zithers, and flutes, unelectrified guitars
lowers, then is shut off because a live guitarist has begun to set
on the small raised stage. The waitress stops to look at him, tur
back to me.

Like her co-workers, this child-woman believes in the myth
ogy of food and drink, its force ("John steamed good lentils t
day"), the welcome illusion of Family and Mother Earth, t
business of Food and Man. She pushes hair from her face. "Fo
get the lentil. Go with a green. See your skin? Touch the skin."

I scan my hands, then hers.

"I'm after broccoli . . . going for broccoli," she says, "a plant
the mustard family." She points at the chalkboard menu of sou
Then, hands on her hips: "You didn't know that."

"No." What I mean is I'm not ordering soup.

What she means is the mustard clan. "Well, it is. Brass
oleracea botrytis. Cauliflower too."

"You know Latin then? I knew a woman who knew trees
Latin. A walk in the woods was the same as sitting Mass."

"Cauliflower is just white broccoli."

The waitress heads for the Latin soup she's selected. Her hi
like Barrie's, seem lost in her jeans, which look as if they mig
have been truly washed with stones. She spins to throw a sw
glance my way—Trust Me—her eyes enlarged by youth, meg
vitamins, and the luxury of some single realizable resolve li
Good Soup. Near the door of the open kitchen, she waves for n

attention, taps the chalkboard menu. With her right forefinger and thumb she pinches the flesh of her other raised hand. She clucks her tongue just loud enough for me to hear.

While I wait for the soup, I think of Andrew's wife, Suzanne, the woman before and during Barrie. I think to send Suzanne a greeting card from among the restaurant's large stock: a portrait of Frank Lloyd Wright. Or James, Henry James. A young and tanned Picasso. Photo reductions of the works of Henry Moore. An empty upholstered chair gazing seaward from Dover Beach. *Ah, love, let us be true.*

If I had a card depicting a three-wheeled Italian truck, carrying (strapped down with clothesline cord) a blood-red velvet couch, sheets and pillows, huge bedposts and a mirror, I would mail the card, beg Suzanne to move from Utah. I would promise her *Poor Richard's*, expressed and scurried love, clement weather. The Italian truck in the card would be parked on a cobbled street. There would be a dun-colored, flat-fronted building in the back and a half-raised, corrugated, gray metal door.

The waitress delivers thick soup and thick bread, then hands me a spoon with a sergeant's look, sits at my table.

I shovel up a load. The soup tastes distressingly healthy, but I admit to myself that eating it can't be all bad. I work on the soup until my waitress reminds me she's brought bread. I dip a hunk of it like a spoon, then eat it. The waitress stands proud: "There you go."

I comment on the generous restocking of the book shelves.

"Heine says," my waitress says, touching a book spine, "*People who burn books will burn people.* Heine *said*, I guess. He's gone—he used to write letters to Karl Marx."

The waitress ticks a memory of Marx and I recall reading something like one man's hour is not worth another man's hour—rather, one man during an hour is worth just as much as another man during an hour. In Marx's world, though, contradictorily, time is all, man nada. "He is at most," Marx also wrote, "time's carcass."

I feel my Marx quote as close to accurate as the one from Heine but don't trouble the waitress with it. Barrie would have given the college-aged waitress credit enough for putting to memory one smart someone's thoughts.

The long-sleeved T-shirt the waitress wears displays what looks to be a Philip Guston reproduction: white-hooded and booted figures. The T-shirt, like her pants, hangs large. She seems happy I'm eating. I offer a piece of bread for her to dip.

"Don't worry, I eat plenty." She plants a hand on her dancer's stomach, settles back in the chair. People get up themselves for beer or for coffee, drop money on the counter, figure change. When I've finished my soup, my waitress gathers my bowl and plate, sweeps crumbs, then carts everything to the kitchen. In this absence, I move Barrie's mother's letters from the table to my coat.

My waitress returns with a glass for herself and two beers. She has pushed down her sleeves. Her lips are still pale, unpainted, but she now ports rings on all fingers. She sees me looking, fans her hands.

"I'm Deidra," she says, throws her arms towards the ceiling. "I *like* my name."

Before I finish the beer in my glass, Deidra refills from my new bottle. She bugs her eyes at me: "Hard to quit my shift." She tells me I liked the soup, then tells me I should try the day's coffee.

"I'll finish the beer."

"It's all right," she says, heading for the kitchen. "If it gets cold, I'll fix it."

Back, she waits while I taste the coffee.

"Good? I know. If it cools, I'll shove it in the microwave— disturb it at the molecular level."

"You attend the college?"

She doesn't push away from the table, but removes her hands, drops them to her lap. "I put in two things of cream. Those dwarf cups."

My waitress, Deidra, turns her chair to watch and to hear the music. The guitarist, who I see is as old as I, has begun to warm a flute.

I hand Deidra money for a beer for the musician. Deidra sits beside him. She points and the guitarist salutes.

When I lift my own beer, my hand shakes, so I set the bottle down without filling my glass. Then there's noise from the kitchen. Above the head of the handsome cook rinsing sprouts is tacked a notice for employees to wash their hands, which I can read from where I sit. Someone has penned beneath the state's orders, in fat black script: *And water for our kids?*

Barrie Hooper's dead.

Of the letters I sent, none had worked. What were my letters but an unsound trust in wit and conversation? Barrie was so nimbly beautiful and funny that I'd worked to believe, over time, that she was settled and in love with me. Like most men, I had things reversed. Remember the John Travolta line in *Saturday Night Fever*—"You fuck a girl and she expects you to dance with her"? Everything backasswards, muddied.

Barrie would have ordered avocados and beer. To me: "*Persea Americana*, a tropical American fruit, also called *alligator pear*." To Deidra: "This is my second time in Colorado. I was here when I was twelve. You should wear lipstick. You have a bonny mouth, a *perfecto* mouth—no one's said?"

Barrie would have purchased a cowboy shirt. Across the table where Diedra has been, I see an afterimage of Barrie. Her new shirt is red.

Despite months and gallons of paint, *Poor Richard's* still smells of smoke.

From across the street, two uniformed guards measure us from behind a barred iron gate, a barn-sized opening in the stone wall that defends this residence of a foreign legation. The wall rises so that all we see above it are the dormers of the great house, the pepperbox turrets, slate roof, tops of oaks. Old oak behind the wall and along both curbs canopy the street, and here, just off Connecticut Avenue in Washington, D.C., it seems near dark. The foreign guards stand a step behind the barred gate, baby-cradling army green weapons. In the shadow of a porched door, I now see a third armed person. Above the main entrance a flag: a half moon and star, a green field.

Before I park, Barrie's out of the car, standing on the curb with her basket. I get out, lock both sides of the rental. Barrie's sitting on the curb with the basket. Soon as I round the car, she parades her stash: two bottles of wine, silver, china, glasses, napkins. "*Linen* napkins," Barrie says, then stands. She hands me the basket.

From our side of things, Barrie now starts to let the arme guards have it. "Hey, *Glasnost!*" she shouts, then steps towar the gate.

"Those guards look Pakistani, not Russian, so don't. Take look at the flag—no sickle. The flag's green. It must be Pakistar so stop." The flag flaps in light wind.

"They wall us out like it's not our city." Barrie points toward the top of the wall where we see what looks like embedded glass shards like stuck leaves. She starts in again. "Hey! The fine fo animal sacrifice in the U.S. is a thousand bucks!" She points bac at the glass. "For scooping kneecaps. Palms."

I herd Barrie down the street to Connecticut Avenue, the pivot her towards KOSMOS, the deli she'd asked me to stop for.

"Had more facts for them," Barrie says, squinting back at th wall and gate. "I collect them."

"You do? Collect *this*: half the terrorist victims worldwide ar Pakistani. You think they don't keep count? When those guard moved to the gate, they moved like they were ready to fire. Di they know what you had in your basket? Smarten up."

"Hey," Barrie says. "Lighten up."

"Don't tempt armed guards in their own walled yards. They' shoot you, Barrie. *Fact.*"

"This is some city, right? People swapping facts like bribes o wives—*statistics*. You have numbers, you can, you know, ma neuver—condemn, bless, accuse, instruct. I have this trap min for facts." Then: "How many nude women accepted Domino' Pizza deliveries last year in this town?" She doesn't wait for m guess: "*Fifteen*."

"Advertise that, you'll put Americans out of work, what witl armed Pakistanis moonlighting, delivering pizza." Then: "Fifteer sounds low."

But Barrie waves me off, stoops to block a brindled bulldog making his way towards us, rear end sashaying: a car on ice. H has a six-foot branch in his chops. The owner, a lean, short haired woman in a jogging suit, catches up, ropes the dog's unat tached leash around her own neck. Though fit as a runner, she' not wearing running shoes; she wears rubber Wellingtons.

"What's your name, Big Boy?" Barrie asks, on her knees roughing it up with the dog. With both hands she jerks at th branch, starts growling herself. She stops to consider the owner. "What's his name?"

"I put a pink collar on her and people still ask what's his name."

"You're a girl—you want to look like this?" Barrie takes the dog's block face in her hands, shakes it back and forth, the flews and dewlaps flapping, tilts it up. "Not me," says Barrie. She knocks on the woman's Wellingtons, like two rubber doors. "What's with the boots?"

The Captain hums into the intercom—a good old boy—*Let's fasten our belts, friends.* He informs the attendants to be seated. The plane is punched again. The seat belt sign flickers off, then on. At 33,000 feet, the sky is bright and cloudless. Passengers crane to hear the Captain, peer with bewilderment through portholes. What they see is blue sky, sun.

Captain Miracle reports he has clearance *to fly above the stuff.* Seat belts cinched, everyone looks up. The plane does not rise, then does. At 39,000 feet, the sky is bright and cloudless, and the Captain discourses upon clear-air turbulence. His point seems to be to keep the lecture light, but there is reverence in his twang. Then he releases the attendants to serve drinks.

While I wait for a drink, I open a magazine to a two-page color ad—a commercial pimping of The End: *Second Coming, Inc.*: books, jewelry, luggage, coffee mugs (*Give Your Heart to Jesus*), cassettes, videos, bumper stickers (*God Bless Our Camper*), sweatshirts, iron-ons, paperweights, stained glass (*Get Saved—Or Else!*), pencils, pens, toys (a good-sized plastic whale with a removable human).

The woman beside me, the one on the aisle, slaps my page, rolls her eyes, whistles through her teeth. Behind us, a child shrieks. I tense, as though the child knows something, but the airplane sails, unmolested.

Across the aisle, three men flirt with a leggy stew. One of them speaks to her in crummy German. The stewardess speaks to the man in accented but intact English. The man repeats himself in high-school German. My German is good enough to understand.

You keep your urge to defend a pretty woman, but the one beside me shakes her head: "Stewardesses are enough armed. Talk to me. Order *me* a drink. My name is *Barrie*."

The stewardess asks the man, who is speaking up again, to repeat himself in English. He repeats himself in German. She asks, "Why do you wish to exclude your friends?" Barrie hoists her shoulders: *See?*

The German stewardess serves Barrie and me our drinks. Barrie tells me she works in an office that publishes a journal for the Department of Defense. In Washington, she says, everyone works for the Department of Defense.

"Pretty pat, huh? Too pat?"

"Not at all. No."

Later, as we descend into National Airport, Barrie points at the lighted Pentagon: "*Home*."

We are close enough to the ground that the earth is speeding, but I can see that Arlington National Cemetery and the Pentagon almost touch. The contours of the two shrines clash—the cemetery fleshy loops, the Pentagon bony, as though its success has made it immobile and its *stabilis* now exalted over all other virtues.

Captain Miracle feathers the engines, eases into the chocks. He instructs us to remain in our seats, then, like a teacher at the bell, works in a final fact: *This is the nation's capital.* Barrie eyes the intercom.

In the terminal, she writes down her phone number. She knows I'm attending a conference that is to run four days. She holds her phone number up: "You can't be busy for four *full* days. I don't believe you."

I watch the hang of her dress, the summer cotton. "Call then," she says. She doesn't bother to turn. "*Call me*."

During the flight from Colorado, Captain Miracle asked us to peer down—*just off to your right, now*—thousands of feet to see the St. Louis Cardinals' baseball park. Barrie unbuckled her belt. Draped across me, she gazed towards the earth. "Where? There?"

Now seated in *Poor Richard's*, I remember. She hangs over a while, then: "I watch baseball once a year. The last game of the World Series."

"How do you know which game is the last?"

"You know."

"How would you unless it's the seventh?"

"Seventh?"

"Game. Final game. The seventh."

"Doesn't matter," Barrie says.

"Sure it does."

"Why would it matter? My system works fine for me. Give it air."

At the door of the deli, Barrie takes the basket I'd picked up while she'd played with the dog. "Wellingtons are named for Arthur Wellesley."

"And they're not called Wellesleys?"

"Wellesley the Duke," she says. "Of *Wellington*," she says— "Waterloo? Prime Minister?" She next supplies dates: "1815. 1828. I told you," she says, taps her skull. "If they're low-caste guards, they're probably eunuchs. They might as well give up any plans of delivering pizza. I named her Ophelia."

I raise both hands to slow Barrie down. "Ophelia the dog, the girl bulldog?"

"The dog, sure, *and* . . . Hamlet's squeeze, right? Hamlet's girlfriend. She went nuts. Probably she saw too much. In the play, she goes nuts." Barrie tells me her favorite T-shirt is one she bought at a Shakespeare Festival in New York. "I read the play in school, but New York's where I saw it—outdoors, under stars." She says her picture T-shirt of Shakespeare is captioned Will Power. "Ophelia drowns herself," Barrie says, "but when they pull her from the pond to cart her on stage, why isn't she wet and muddy? She's coifed. She's clean and dry. She's covered with petals."

Inside KOSMOS, Barrie's deli, I sort through a freezer of ice cream. Each small carton has a packaged wooden spoon attached with an elastic. Finally, I pick a flavor by the color of its package—the Danish or Swedish labelings look to me like defaced

Latin, dots and slashes. Armed with a burgundy carton, I crane, then head for Barrie.

I have eight ounces of ice cream; Barrie has challah bread, German salad, a kiwi, a fat orange, a container of herring, and is leaning at the counter asking about cheese. Barrie shows the clerk the bottles of red wine in her basket. She tells him we're on our way to Wolf Trap, that Rostropovich is doing that Shostakovich thing with his symphony, but she calls it his *band*. She makes cartoon eyes: "For whatever they say, those commies glaum close."

"Shostakovich was harassed his entire career, harassed till he died. Rostropovich is a naturalized U.S. citizen, Barrie. One of us."

Barrie points behind the clerk at an uncut wheel of Camembert. The clerk taps at some cut Brie under the glass of the counter, then points at Barrie's wine, nodding yes.

Barrie mouths yes in French, intently involving her lips. I aim for the lips with the ice cream.

Barrie bites at the spoon: "Stop. How much Brie do we need? Stop. Tell me."

The clerk hefts a good-sized wedge, looks at me.

"We'll take it."

"It's seven dollars a pound, Stephen, so no. Maybe half that."

"It's our anniversary, OK? We'll take it."

"Your anniversary? Serious?" The clerk traps a co-worker. Her hair is dark, cropped short.

"You hear that?" the clerk asks the girl. "An anniversary. How about a little kiss for Phil?" The cropped-haired girl pecks at Phil. But when Phil tries to kiss her, the girl pulls away. When that happens, Phil bends to wrap the cheese.

Barrie knocks hard on the glass of the counter. "We'll take half that. What didn't you hear? Didn't you hear me?" Phil parts the Brie.

I go ahead and taste the ice cream. "I'm throwing the ice cream in." Behind his counter, Phil backs a step, raises his hands: "Your anniversary. Your day."

Barrie leans to pull Phil to her, plants a kiss on his face.

"Hey. Yeah," Phil says, rings up our bill, starts to bag our food, then stops to pack the food into Barrie's basket, then talks Barrie into a third bottle of wine: a Romanian red, a bargain. He checks to see we have utensils. "This is something. Hey. How long has it been?" he directs at me. "The anniversary and all?"

"Depends on whether you count from the wedding or when we first moved in."

Phil motions us away from the registers and the cropped-haired girl to the end of the counter. Here are tall open jars of black and green olives, and, under the counter glass, fresh pasta.

"Tell me," Phil starts. "Before you moved in, did you wonder if you should? You were sure about it when you did it?"

I reach to pull Barrie close. When she resists, I can feel her ribs. "We're not married, and we haven't lived together. This is our first date."

"Second," says Barrie. She wants to count the day before when we met on the plane. "Look," Barrie'd said as we'd approached D.C., "you're on vacation, but I'm home. I'll pick you up tomor-row—tell me where." Barrie bumps me now with her hip. "Say second."

"Look," I tell Phil, "you're serious, and I'm horsing around. I was horsing around."

"Say second."

Phil hoists his brows and both hands. "You had me, man, know it?" He extends a hand. "Hey."

"I'll see you, Phil." I shake the hand. "Hey."

"I'm not Phil." The clerk points at the girl. "That's Phil," he says. "She's Phyllis."

At Wolf Trap, Barrie and I recline on the grass, which slopes towards the park's large and covered, but temporary, stage. There's been a suspicious fire, following which the permanent stage has been torn down. Before the curtains rise, a park official makes an official plea for donations. He calls the Wolf Trap Farm Park the National Symphony's home-away-from-home, and a national treasure.

When the Canadians—five guest brass players—and the con-ductor ("Ros-tro-**po**-vich," Barrie had said, "say it like that, but fast: Rostro**po**vich") have exited for the third and last time, people start folding their chairs and blankets. Barrie and I stay put on her quilt. While we watch people leave, we uncork the third bottle of wine, the bargain. Scraps of our picnic are still around us. In time, most of the lights are cut, the starred sky brightens, and a park ranger appears. He suggests we leave before the parking lots are locked. He eyes our litter but acts unnaturally civil, touches the stiff brim of his hat—a ranger salute—marches off. The beam of his flashlight jounces.

Soon, no more car headlamps flare up from the lots.

"He looked about six," says Barrie.

We look up to see sky. The stars seem close but dim, the sky small. I tell Barrie that stars in the West are bigger. She doesn' know I was raised in Montana, but she knows where I live now is Colorado. I tell her I know what I'm talking about. "In the moun tains, the sky's huge. Ungauzed." I squeeze my eyes tight shut to recall.

Barrie says she and her family once camped, when she wa young, in Estes Park—Rocky Mountain National Park—in Colo rado. Sleeping outside the family station wagon, she'd watched the sky all night she says. "That's right, *all* night."

Barrie says she remembers the West—the pines, the *Populu tremuloides*: quaking aspen, the mountains, the camel-colored desert—and that her father, the government horticulturist, ha not demanded of her and her sisters the Latin names of Wester plants. She asks me to drive one day to the National Arboretur in the District, where she will name trees for me and for he father—*the factual, living father*, she says—"In Latin," she say then sits up.

Hitching her shawl, Barrie spills wine in her lap. The bargai wine spreads red on her white trousers. I leap away, safe. Barr mops up with a corner of the quilt.

When Barrie's all done, I sit down.

"It's not funny," she says.

I refill Barrie's glass, then arrange the shawl for her. It's sum mer, but cold. The quilt feels damp from the grass. The corn Barrie has used to mop with looks black.

Barrie says she bought the quilt for five dollars at a garage sa in Bethesda. She says it was mildewed when she bought it. soaked it in white vinegar, then purified water, then line dried and see? You know what to do if you spill dark wine on a rug? You pour salt on the wine, then let the salt dry, then vacuum."

Through a torn patch in Barrie's quilt, I see, even in moonlight, what seems a stitched panel underneath, not batting. Barrie says she didn't know about the covered quilt until the covering quilt tore. I wonder aloud whether the first quilt was recovered or an effort of unseen work, secret love?

"Like I know?" asks Barrie. "I would know?"

I point to the windbreak of trees which backs the breast of the hill where we sit. All at once we lean back, peering up over our heads. The trees loom like full masts.

"*Quercus alba*," Barrie says, "White oak." Then: "Do you know constellations?" By this time, we're flat on our backs.

"The only constellation I know is the moon."

"The moon is not a constellation."

When I try to kiss Barrie, she moves.

We stop for beers at CAPTAIN KIRK'S, a music bar in Barrie's Maryland suburb. CAPTAIN KIRK'S disc jockey, surrounded by gear and light, could be Shatner at his console. When he stands, I see his T-shirt. The shirt is black imprinted in silver with a reproduction of the Milky Way. I point at the shirt: "*Galaxias Kyklos.* 'Circle of Milk.' Milky Way."

"That's not Latin," Barrie says, then squints to see. She has had to turn in her seat to look. She roots in her purse for glasses.

"It's Greek. I just wanted to say it: '*Galaxias Kyklos.*'" What it says on the T-shirt, with an arrow pointing near the center of the arc of the stars and the star dust, is: YOU ARE HERE. I tell Barrie.

Barrie stops digging for her glasses. When she looks up, she has narrowed her eyes. "Must be nice to know where you are and wear the map." Then: "I've tried to kill myself. I started at sixteen. I had a sister who tried it first. She drank Drano. It ruined her mouth and her throat—*esophagus*, my father would say. They tubed her *esophagus* with plastic or something, space-age something. She lives on liquids through a tube, but she's pretty much fucked things."

While I stare, Barrie takes a good, deep breath, waves me off. "Forget I said that," she says. "Forget I said it."

"Hey." I snap off corners of one of a stack of felt coasters that have been left with our mugs. "This stuff is what? crushed dust. glued dust? safe asbestos or something?" The coasters bear the likenesses of the USS *Enterprise* and enemy ships.

Barrie points at the disc jockey, who's donning a Washington Redskins cap, replacing the blue NASA cap he'd had on. When we'd walked in, Barrie had stood in a spot of light, her blooded trousers drawing stares. She'd stood and pointed at the disc jockey's cap, explaining that NASA Headquarters was but a mile away. "We could walk there," she said. Barrie said NASA was where her father worked before he retired. "Plants for space," she'd explained. "Plants for oxygen, plants for food, plants for companionship."

"Plants are our friends," I said.

"You think you're funny?" Barrie said.

"My oldest sister," Barrie now says, "was a nurse who didn't come home from Song Trang. My sister's on The Wall in the city. My family could have an arrow there. Like his." Barrie repeats what I've told her is written on the disc jockey's shirt. "YOU ARE HERE," she says. "The Wall's our place. My family has its arrow. *There.*" She points towards D.C. The wall she points through is dotted with photos: Spock, Bones, Scottie, male and female Klingons, and the man himself: James Tiberius Kirk.

"Do you know what she said when the doctor asked why?"

I have to guess Barrie means the sister who drank the Drano.

"She said she didn't know it would hurt so much." Then: "I have a sister who's dead and a sister with a throat like a bottle." Barrie lofts her beer.

"Humans don't survive as a race, or families as families, Barrie. Individual people do. Individuals survive, not species."

"I ought to write that down," Barrie says. "I ought to get that down on paper. You sound like a fucking talk show. By the by, you've got it turned round—the species survives, not persons. I had a physics class the year I turned sixteen that I hated." Barrie turns her hands, wrists up. "No. Pills," she says, turns them back. "If you really want to kill yourself," Barrie says, "you can."

Barrie says she wants more beer, so I raise a hand towards a waitress tables away, extend two fingers, then point at our table.

rest my arm in the air because it feels hooked there. I have to will it down.

"I swallow my parents' pills, then I puke their pills, then I forget and flush their toilet. By the time my parents come home I'm undressed and in bed, my own bed. I meant to be asleep in their closet."

When the waitress arrives—this time with chilled mugs and bottled beer—Barrie stops talking to pour. I lift my bottle to drink, but Barrie takes it from me, then tilts my new mug to fill it. I touch the thin lid of foam, announce that beer foams up a storm in Colorado: "Thin air. High-altitude air. Loosened air or something."

"Stick your finger in your beer when you pour. It won't foam," Barrie says. She sticks her finger in my beer.

When I reach for her hand, Barrie jerks it away, spills my mug. "Barrie," I say. "No, listen." But Barrie covers her ears.

With a coaster edge I squeegee beer to the floor.

Barrie uncovers her ears.

I start. "Hollywood's filming this movie in India—OK?—and they're building these fake slums. The movie's this movie about this Indian rickshaw puller and a Catholic priest in the Calcutta slums. The movie-set slums are so authentic—tin and mud and wood shacks—that at night, when the crews aren't filming, people start moving in. *Actual* people, Barrie, not actors. So they build this fence around the movie slums to keep real people from moving in, but when the movie's done—and this is *the part*, the part I want you to hear—Hollywood-tears-down-the-slums. People have camped outside this fence for months—they've been *waiting*. Hollywood leaves, but destroys these fifty-two new slum houses. Calcutta has three hundred slum neighborhoods and over forty percent of the city's twelve million residents live in slums and Hollywood removes fifty-two perfectly good slum houses."

Barrie clamps her eyes, then pops awake: "Forty percent of twelve million is what? four million?—no, four point eight mil. What's fifty-two houses?"

"It's fifty-two, Barrie, *Five-Two*." I raise fingers on both hands to show.

"You could want me?" Barrie asks. "You think I'm pretty?" Then: "Me?" She lifts her chin as she waits to know.

"If it's one house, then it's one house, Barrie. It counts."

"In the morning, my mother brings in soup. I think, if I eat this soup, I have to live."

"You know something, Barrie? I don't feel drunk. My head should feel like high tide. It doesn't. I don't feel drunk."

"Well, you're drunk."

When Barrie drinks her beer, I watch her throat work. I tell her I'm stringing words like bracelets, pearl bracelets: "*insistence, regality, truculence, unrest, desire, grue.*" I tell her the words arrive lighted. I tell her, "You look like that pretty pro tennis star. You could be her sister. You know, what's-her-name. You're pretty."

"You're drunk."

It seems I should ask some question now, but what?

"By the by," Barrie says, "eunuchs live fourteen years longer, on average, than intact men."

"Some remedy."

Barrie removes a vial from her purse, uncaps it to extract a good-sized pill, which she downs with beer.

"You all right? What's that for?"

"When it mixes with alcohol, it makes me throw up."

"It what?"

"I'm-not-supposed-to-be-drinking-the-pill-will-make-me-throw-up."

"You mean now?"

Barrie closes her eyes, pushes back, as though traveling, a long flight. There is in her posture an athletic clarity, purpose, fury. Sweat pearls on her forehead and upper lip: linked full moons, constellations.

I force myself to turn to face the captain of this ship and his stereo speakers. Our disc jockey has stood on his lighted dais. He reaches high to stretch, then to bow at the waist, touch the floor. He palms the floor, but he cheats at the knees. As he holds this pose, his cap topples off. He has a bald spot the size of a saucer.

When the disc jockey unbends, he catches me watching. He replaces his cap, then thumps his chest and the spiral galaxy. He runs a finger along the shaft of the pointing arrow. X marks the spot: YOU, he points to Barrie and me then back, ARE HERE. Certain of our place in the heavens, he waves hello.

Twenty
Ways
to
Look
at
Fire

fire (fīr) *n.,v.* -*n.* the state, process, or instance of combustion in which ignited fuel or other material combines with oxygen, giving off light, heat, and flame. -*v.t.* to bake, as in a kiln; to cause to burn. -*v.i.* to be kindled; flame up; glow. [ME; OE *fyr;* c. Icel *furr,* G *Feuer,* Gk *pyr* (see PYRO-)]

fire, one of man's essential tools, control of which helped start him on the path toward civilization. Peking man, living about 500,000 B.C., is the first confirmed fire user, though he was, no doubt, a fire *tender,* rather than fire *maker*—the first fires undoubtedly the effect of lightning. It took a half million years for man to convincingly harbor fire, as well as develop a rudimentary agriculture and stone tools. About 7000 B.C., Neolithic man acquired reliable fire-making techniques: that is, friction-producing implements or flint and pyrites. Techniques have been improved.

1. There is little evidence among Germans of widespread refusal to cooperate with the Nazis. Beyond this, the British Foreign Office and the U.S. State Department turned down rescue plans that would have saved numbers of Jews from the furnaces. A large number of the murdered European Jews were burned.

2. In May 1963, Buddhists, demonstrating in Hue against persecution by the Diem regime, were fired on by government police. On June 11, a monk set himself aflame at a major intersection in downtown Saigon. This act, tipped off to an AP reporter, was recorded and the photo flashed about the world. The incident drew attention.

3. *For, behold, the Lord will come with his chariots like a whirlwind, to render his anger with fury and his rebuke with flames of fire.*

4. The two-day incendiary raid by more than 2,000 Allied bombers ignited a firestorm that consumed the city of Dresden, claiming 135,000 German souls. The medieval Dresden was the home of Europe's first china. The making of pottery is an ancient art, though not overly ancient, because it requires a banked and tended fire. In firing, the moisture in the clay is removed.

5a. Firebombing in Japan during World War II was in particular effective, but required many bombers and many bombs. A firebombing sortie called for up to as many as 300 bombers, each carrying, at war's end, an average of 7.4 tons of bombs. Enola Gay, by contrast, carried one crew and one bomb over Hiroshima. "Little Boy," the atomic bomb lowered on Hiroshima, was the approximate size of a ten-foot man weighing 9,000 pounds. "Little Boy" killed 70,000 people.

5b. "Fat Man" wasn't scheduled for Nagasaki. About the same length as "Little Boy," though rounder and heavier, "Fat Man" was to be air burst above Kokura, but weather preserved the city. The Superfortress spent ten minutes over Kokura without sighting its aim point, then proceeded to the secondary target of Nagasaki. Though the plutonium-based "Fat Man's" destructive potential exceeded that of the uranium-based "Little Boy," the hilly terrain of Nagasaki restricted damage: a few over 30,000 expired.

6. An exterminating weapon of choice employed by Allied forces in their battles against the last-ditch resistance of the Japanese in the Pacific islands was the flame thrower. The portable version, carried on the backs of ground troops, had a range of forty-five yards and enough fuel for ten seconds of continuous fire. Larger units installed in tank turrets doubled the range and could carry enough fuel for a burst of up to sixty seconds. Because these instruments, portable or no, projected streams of oil burning at temperatures of two thousand degrees Fahrenheit, mere seconds of use proved enough. They were especially effective against Japanese defending caves and coconut bunkers.

7. The practice of cremation on open fires was introduced as early as 1000 B.C. The *Iliad* refers to the royal cremation of the hero Hector. Achilles was incinerated following seventeen days of lavish mourning. Cremation in western Europe became rare, however, except during emergencies such as plague years. In 1656, for instance, sixty thousand plague victims were burned in Naples in a single week. Modern cremation has evolved beyond open fires. Bodies are placed in chambers where concentrated heat transforms them in sixty minutes to a few pounds of powder.

8. Napalm is a petroleum gel that is ignited by contact and burns prolongedly. Because napalm is a jelly, it affixes to what it burns. Napalm was developed by Harvard University scientists.

9. An estimate of the force of the firestorm in Dresden can be obtained by analyzing it as a meteorological phenomenon: as a result of the sudden linking of a number of fires, the air above is heated to such an extent that a violent updraft occurs, which, in turn, causes surrounding fresh air to be sucked in from all sides. This suction causes movements of air far greater than normal winds. In meteorology, the differences of temperature involved to create wind current are on the order of $20°$ to $30°$ C. In the Dresden firestorm, the temperature differences were on the order of $600°$ to $1000°$ C. This explains the liveliness of firestorm winds.

10. Oświęcim, better known by its German name, Auschwitz— or, more properly, Auschwitz-Birkenau—is a small town in

southern Poland. Established in 1940, the camp was, for five years, a model of efficient work. At its peak, the death camp's *Badean-stalten* ("bath houses") accommodated two thousand people at once. Twelve thousand inmates could be processed per day. With its numerous and orderly prison blocks, gas chambers, and crematoria, Oświęcim covered but fifteen square miles, though two million or so people were there housed and exterminated. Once murdered, the method of the disposal of Jews was fire. Generally, the inmates were worked to death or starved, though qualified Nazi doctors performed medical experiments on a select few.

11. The total mass of the fragments of a split atom is usually less than the combined mass of the original nucleus and the bombarding neutron. The missing mass, m, is transformed into energy, E, in accordance with Einstein's equation $E=mc^2$, where c is the velocity of light. Because the velocity of light is so large (186,000 miles per second), a small amount of mass corresponds to an enormous amount of energy. This explains the small size but large effects of atomic bombs.

12. The firebombing of Dresden took place on February 13–14, 1945. February 14, 1945, was not only St. Valentine's Day, but was the seventh Wednesday before Easter and the first day of Lent—that is, *Ash Wednesday*, the day on which many Christians receive a mark of ashes on their foreheads as a token of penitence and mortality.

13. The amount of energy released in the process of fission is so great that the complete fission of 1.5 pounds of uranium or plutonium would create the equivalent of the explosive energy of 24 million pounds of TNT. One characteristic of the atomic bomb is the high temperature it spawns. The maximum temperature at the bursting point reaches several million degrees. The energy of thermal radiation is about 35 percent of the whole energy of the bomb. An enormous amount of energy of about 7×10^{12} calories is, therefore, released as thermal radiation from a standard atomic bomb. Thermal radiation affects flesh.

14. By way of vindication and excuse, it has been pointed out that the horrifying atomic bomb death toll in Hiroshima was in fact somewhat less than that occasioned five months before by the patterned dropping of ordinary incendiary bombs on Tokyo. In a single night, one-fourth of the city was torched, one million

made homeless, and some number over eighty thousand citizens burned. The core temperature of Tokyo ranged from 1,000 to 2,000 degrees Fahrenheit. Water in the city's canals boiled.

15. Firebombing is efficient, as approximately 85 percent of the weight of a firebomb is fuel.

16. *I am come to send fire on the earth; and what will I, if it be already kindled?*

17. In 1945, *The New York Times* ran a picture ad for a U.S. chemical company. The ad displayed a GI blasting a path "through stubborn Jap defenses" with a flame thrower. "Clearing Out a Rat's Nest," the *Times* captioned the photo.

18. The power of the atomic bomb comes from the forces holding each atom of substance together.

19. In six months of firebombing, starting with the Tokyo raid, civilian casualties in Japan doubled those suffered by the Japanese military worldwide in forty-five months of war. By the time "Little Boy" and "Fat Man" struck, B-29s had triumphantly firebombed five dozen Japanese cities.

20. Cremation has returned to fashion. Many Protestant churches actively support cremation as a principal form of burial. The Roman Catholic church has lifted its prohibition. The Jewish religion continues to forbid it.

Fire Road

The winter Alexandra was in her second year of high school and newly possessed of a driving permit, a heater hose in the old Datsun burst. Twenty years, and I'm stuck with that part of that day. *Sky looks greasy, pressured for storm. Air like suet. 4 P.M. Cold.*

Alex had expected to drive to SAFEWAY, been headed for the wheel. "You think we don't have snow on the roads at school? We had to watch a zillion flicks. Snow flicks. I'm driving."

The slab where I parked the Datsun had been coated from storms, ice fattening for weeks. The night temperature had so steadfastly nicked zero that the mark had become a temperature you could believe in, a *location*. Like the inside of a bell. The interior of a cathedral.

The slab ice only melted from the heat of a just-parked car. Each morning I backed the Datsun out, I saw the shell restored. In the mornings the ice looked permanent. Now, spreading from beneath the car, was unfreezable muck. The leaked antifreeze had the look of clabber.

"What is it?" Alex asked. "What's that?"

"Don't step in it."

"What is it?"

"Get your feet out of it, Alex. Go in."

"I need lunch. I'm not buying at school." She was back toeing the spill.

"I told you, go in."

"I need stuff."

I sat Alex on the porch. "Sit down." I unlaced my sixteen-year-old's boots, then pulled them, then pointed at the door. She went in.

In the yard, I stuffed my hands into Alex's boots, then toed them in the snow to clean them. Then I straightened. There was still a good hour of day, but the sky looked brighter than it seemed it should have, as though the day's temperature had altered light. I listened for noise, but the cold had made everything quiet. I took the time just to stand there, shut my eyes. Alex interrupted from the porch. She wanted her boots. I kept the boots on my hands. She shut the door.

The yellow-green pool under the car had worked its way now around a tire, and I watched as if I expected the muck to climb and work the rubber: dog-hungry, brained glop from some raw planet on a search. I so disliked the sight of my carport ice defiled that I called up the clean vision of an Arctic fox I'd spied one winter in Alaska's Brooks Range, just north of the Arctic Circle. It was a healthy male whose coat should have shone fox silver, yet there he sped, terra-cotta against unmarked snow. That spell, lasting but seconds, had remained one of the permanent visions of my life: a beauty I felt in unblessed surrender to the spill of antifreeze beneath my car. In that unvirtuous green (reflecting a decaying undercarriage), I faced what seemed a further and containing vision of the swift destruction of the North after piled centuries of pure extreme fragile life: my red fox, miles upon miles of what had seemed my own owned ice (unearthly white and pale sky blue unending), perfected storm. And in summer: rock, sun, thaw, rain, hail, illogical flowers, gnats, nervy salmon, caribou, bear. After all the years, my year in the North still counted.

I clapped Alex's boots as much for noise as to jar snow, then tossed them at the porch. Alex cracked open the door, took them. I raised the car's hood, peered in, dropped the hood. Still, as if capable of something, I stared again at lost bile beneath a salt-rimed car—seemingly motionless but rotting steel: wild molecular alteration—and worried for the earth's simple, ungravelled glaciers and for the Arctic, for the scarred tundra above the DEW Line (where I'd spent that year scanning USAF radar for Russian bombers), for the sweet moss there, all the water, the unexpected birds, my racing fox whose fiery coat had skipped (for me?) an entire change of season.

With a long look at the waxed sky, I moved to the house. Inside, I arranged Alex's and my boots on the doormat. The expensive heated air in my house flushed my face.

I called Milo, my mechanic.

"Pump? Hose?"

"Hose."

He started questions about location and damage.

"Milo, Christ."

"All right," Milo said, "no biggie."

"What's that?"

"I said no big thing," Milo said.

"No, you said, 'no biggie.' *Biggie*?"

"Whatever, chum."

Milo was a neighbor, two houses down, but we'd not met until we both played a short season in a city ball league, neither of us lasting the summer—me lost to a knee, Milo to a shoulder that dislocated whenever he swung for anything that would clear second base. We next met for weekly card games with a half-dozen other amateur cripples. At these games, we slammed professional athletes with talent but no heart—named them—shuffled, dealt, smoked, drank, mentioned women.

Milo smacked a kissing sound into the phone: "In the morning then—on my long way in."

Milo, my mechanic. Milo, who wore message T-shirts summer and winter. T-shirts with advice and graphics. T-shirts depicting parts of women and cars. Milo who scrapped wives and children like used tires. Huge in his unguilt, Milo seemed biblical. Whether or not he thought so for himself, Milo—unenthralled by this profession of husband or father—represented for us around the card table a transcending corrective, a regenerating merge of technology and sex and repair. Redemption. Hope unwrenched by Sentiment or Duty. Blessed be the Loss of Consequence. *Self.* The Gospel per Milo: *You gotta believe. He exists. Otherwise who do you talk to during a blow job?* Hallowed be His Name.

Milo and I agreed on a time for my car in the morning, then he stopped me from hanging up to inform that Brandy, Alex's cocker, would suck her paws and die. He told me to hose down the pill. "Hose it. She'll croak."

"Good, Milo. Thanks."

"The crap kills grass."

"Under snow?"

"Dilute it. I mean it. You'll thank me. In the spring you'd see."

"Good, Milo. Thanks."

"I'm telling you what I know." Then: "Girl trouble is worse than car trouble. Don't forget it. Give thanks. Hose it, chum. Your throw." My mechanic hung up.

It was January, outdoor taps shut off, wrapped against frost, hoses coiled in the cellar. *Hose it?* "My hoses are in the cellar," I remarked into the dead connection. *My throw?* I hung up my end of the phone.

Alex was standing beside the kitchen table with her coat on. Alex rarely visited Anna, but it was in Alex to impersonate her mother, familiar signals skipping in like radio from space.

"Well?" said Alex (Anna's lips, *that* face). "I need lunch."

I moved down the hall to the closet, hung my coat, stuffed my cap and my gloves into the pockets.

Alex followed, stopping long enough at the door to pack her feet in her boots.

I said: "Buy lunch. Do that."

Boots on, Alex turned to look, then faced me. She looked as blank faced as her mother.

"Then go the back way," I said, pointing through the walls o the house towards the ridge. I produced a twenty. "Pay atten tion," I said, framed my lips. "Bring me change," I said. "I expec some."

Alex reached past me to my coat for my woolen cap and gloves She snugged on the cap, pulled on the gloves. Then, stuffing my twenty into my glove on her hand, clopped down the hall and ou the back door. Her boots left a trail on the hardwood.

The ridge was a mile-wide stretch of protected state fores separating RidgeView from the unexpected South Mall. In th RidgeView development, you couldn't buy a garbage can withou okayed plans and committee permission; now, within gunshot we had a mammoth blot of stores constructed on rezoned soil During the sudden construction, there had been arsons—build ing materials and the cab of an unlocked truck. For Grand Open ing, someone painted on a Sears wall (five-foot splash letters tha looked pressed from inside, like sweat): *$ RULES*. The wall soo bore (though patrolled and often recoated) what seemed most o Greater RidgeView's heart's dark core: *Fantasies. Nightmares Feud.* Then, in protest or sympathy, people began dumping actua garbage at the foot of the wall—mostly glass of course (tosse bottles), but really anything that could be chucked from a car Then the carcasses: cats, chickens, a pig, the halved dog.

When that happened, RidgeView's Homeowner's Associatio convened and voted in quorum to detail members of a local busi nessmen's four-wheel driving club to defend the ridge betwee the development and the mall. The businessmen (even thos who lived in other suburbs) drove the ridge in irregular shifts though this presence, nonetheless, had a way of seeming planne and bold and apparent. Plus, the vehicles, dawdling in the wood (and at stoplights in town) on fat tires, universally displaye some proof of the citizen's right to bear arms. Through the win ter, the drivers (in down vests and gloves and the club's orang caps) kept the fire roads clearer than normal, and it has to be sai none of what occurred at the Sears wall ever moved towards ou homes.

Still, I felt a shined guilt for permitting Alex to have headed for the mall on her own, though she had done it plenty of times before. Routinely, she and her friends hiked the ridge in the dark to the movies. I did it myself. On foot, the journey was a safe two miles, round-trip. In a car, on loud pavement, more.

I consulted my watch, then shoved a ham in the oven for supper. I made an early strong drink, then retreated to my study, where I supplemented my salary by writing copy for an out-of-state mail-order catalog: a catalog supplying—*At Rea$onable Cost$*—all needs: *Aquarium Vacuums* **(Raise Healthier Fish!)**, *Reusable Coffee Filters, Hooded Four-Legged Sweatsuits for Dogs, Gorilla Masks, Self-Sticking Personalized Address Labels, Embossers, Cat-Grooming Gloves, Painless Tattoos* **(Lasts for Days!)**, *Umbrella Hats, Shoe Stretchers, FuzzEaters, Do-It-Yourself VELCRO Stripping, Dishwater-Safe Fake Parsley,* and so on.

A friend purchased the Aquarium Vacuum from the company I wrote ad for, and in the process of cleaning his fish tank— *"transforming a tedious and dirty job into a simple, one-handed operation"*—hoovered two fish.

I downed three drinks, played some records, fooled with ads: *Delicate, Elegant—yet Durable—Belgian-like Lace Aprons* **(Made in Peru!)** and *Guaranteed Mildew-Proof Shower Curtains* **(Hospital Tested! No Scrubbing!)**—then began to worry over Alex. It was past six. Dark. Diving for zero.

I cleared my desk, dumped what was left of a drink in the sink. In the living room, I stared through my picture window towards the mall as though between me and it there were not tons of frozen soil and woods, as though the dark were not layered as shale. I imagined Alex dogging straight home, like a promise. Even through the weather-paned storms, I could feel the cold.

I let Alex's Brandy out. She milled about, did her business. I stood guard at the back door, ready to steer her from the front-yard spill, but, uncalled, she returned. I let her in, then dressed for the cold, then set out, myself, for the mall. As I was about to pierce the line of trees, Milo hollered. I stopped to wave. Arms jammed with logs, he tossed his head in response. He yelled something. I shrugged and nodded as though I'd understood. Then he hauled in his wood.

A three-week-old blizzard, become manageable in our yards, remained intact among the pine and scrub oak. The tree-bound drifts had disposed themselves to predictable depths. Crusted by winds and no sun, the snow (in places two and three feet deep) had supported Alex, and I paralleled her steps, cracking through the shell that had afforded my daughter passage. Though I'd dug out another hat and gloves, and had worn my coat, I'd not worn boots. I'd laced up low-quartered, nylon running shoes.

The snow beneath the crust was soft and sucked at my feet and frightened me with its pull. I felt lost as a child. I began to run uphill, but kept crashing through the crust, banging my shins, into my own holes.

Intersecting the lower fire road, I squatted, blowing, in a beaten trail, snow-packed by the passage of the four-wheelers, x-country skiers, winter joggers, sleds. But, night fallen, I had become the single human presence. The trees behind blocked all the houses, and the rising ridge still concealed the mall. For all the civilization I knew existed, I felt alone on what could have been, except for the trees, the Polar Ice Cap.

Though I could not see it, I sensed the rise of the moon. I longed for the arrival of my daughter, striding through the dark to end my search, to lead and take me home. I removed my gloves, stood and shook my trousers. Then, knowing more than feeling, hitched my pants to expose my chipped shins and recalled the news report of the Hungarian religious fanatic who, in madness screaming I AM JESUS CHRIST!, scaled a marble balustrade to attack Michelangelo's *Pietà* with a car mechanic's hammer, cleaving the Madonna's nose, breaking her left arm (milk white marble fingers snapping as the left hand struck the floor) in a Vatican basilica. But the image of the broken Madonna was wrong, the comparison vain: (1) I was no damaged mother, (2) had been impregnated by no god; and (3) my offspring, like anyone's, imperfect. All the same, Mary, too, it sunk in, was a *single parent*, bedazed Joseph a pathetic stand-in. Then this: the bourbon felt back and working, and it was unduly complex to line all the parallels (me and Mary and Anna and Joseph and Alex and Christ), though I was solving something out between my mechanic and the nut Hungarian. I quit to examine my legs. My foolish thrashing in crusted snow had affected no one, not even me. The shins would heal.

Bare handed, I crushed white snow against the wounds, the snow blackening, not altogether unpleasantly, in my hands. But that done, the darkness about me swelled, and my hands went cold, and, hunkering alone in the frozen trail, I would have settled for any sign of another's life other than the trampled snow I bent in: a trace of granola, a butt, an oil leak, the visible track of a bird.

I pictured ravens, then red-winged blackbirds, large as crows. I pictured white ponds. Sloughs. Frozen, ratty cattails. When a blackbird attempted to perch, the cattail snapped. Near frozen inlets, I pictured turtles, on their backs. I stopped myself, took hold, inhaled, rubbed the backs of my hands on my nose. I forced deep breaths, felt things catch in my chest, slow. I wished that I hadn't been drinking.

As a child, snowshoeing in a storm, I had fallen behind my father, and had fallen. The snow gave to the curve of my back and my beetle weight, and I'd bellowed for my father. He tramped back, stooped, grasped my wrists. "Stop flailing. You look foolish," he said. "Like a bug." He held onto my wrists, not to raise me, but to remove my gloves. He shook snow from them. Having bared my hands, he instructed me to choose and unhitch one snowshoe, which I was to use to support my weight as I rolled with it pressed to my chest. It worked, and I stood.

"Now rehitch it."

But my hands were cold and the leather thongs of the snowshoe were frozen. My father ungloved his hands and rehitched the shoe. Then, as if I'd not fallen and I'd not cried and he'd not bent to assist me, my father turned and broke trail.

A father myself (and older by years than mine at the time we'd hiked that snow), I rose and pursued the fire road, knowing it to soon turn and rise in its final, short push for the low summit of our civilized wild ridge. Then there Alex was: Alex and a single bag of food—the size of a year-old child—which she clutched to her chest. She walked, staring down. My heart jumped. Seeing her touched as deep a feeling as I'd ever known gaping at her. The day she'd been born, I'd gaped. Our first time together had been without the mother too—just Alex (weightless in my arms) and me in a corridor in a polished hospital at dawn, in Utah. Then, too, there had been a full moon.

"Alex!"

She called back, then delivered the food.

We marched single file in one of the packed tracks of the road.

Alex said, behind me: "It got late before I knew."

When we turned off the lower fire road and I was stepping, once more, through my own broken snow, Alex said, "You goose, you wore shoes."

In that strip of forest those years ago, I spent only minutes, but they are minutes I recall. I find no help against this. For one thing, how she looked in the forest when I found her and she found me is the way I remember Alex before what was to be not minutes at all, but what yet seems years—but of what? years of what? *commotion*? I've searched for words: virus? voodoo? siege? rage? *plain* rage? And Anna, cashing in with advice: "What are you doing about this? My God. Where's she buying it? Is she buying it? I've heard about this." Anna, the mother: *I've heard about this.* "My guess is you need to talk. Do you talk?"

Anna, who presented full-color photos as proof of the end of our marriage. Polaroids: impossible postures in the cameraman's kitchen, on the counters. Anna now leaned at her ease in the remembered kitchen.

"Who took these?" I pretended to study the photos, but was staring more at the same Mixmaster in each print, the stocked knife block, the flecked grain of the Formica, than at naked Anna.

I fanned the photos like a losing hand at Milo's. "Who took these?"

Anna looked at me. I thought of a closed water tap, slapped my cards down.

Anna pointed to a dark car in the driveway. "You don't know him."

Her bags had been packed. She horsed them from the closet to the door, to the driveway. She came back for the third, then got all three in the trunk. The driver didn't get out to load them.

Before Anna and her friend had even backed into the street, I had positioned myself at our kitchen counter. The man I didn't know was tall.

Anna returned in a week for a week, but she left again. This second time she left with a U-HAUL. She took plenty. "Fair is fair" was the original way she put it (one of a dozen notes in the kitchen). Not that I would have stopped her. *Fair is fair*. But the way she made the haul (I was at work, Alex at school), she copped the credit cards from the desk and, the same day, withdrew what there was of savings.

She bought a two-door, two-tone Camaro—vinyl roof, bucket seats, a forgotten Eagles tape—and on the credit cards, a series of refrigerator-freezers, which she then sold at discount for cash, her investment the cost of the classified ads. Good old Anna. Motherly Anna. "What does she do all night when she's out? Have you asked her, Stephen? Why don't you sound more nervous? Don't you think you should sound more nervous?"

Anna, whose big idea had been LA: "You've picked an awful time to call."

"In the afternoon—the middle of the afternoon?"

"Was that a joke? You're a laugher."

"You've tabbed me, Anna—I'm a card."

"It's important for you to believe I spend all my time in the sack like I'm some sort of sex crook. Why is that?" Then: "Are you drinking? You are."

"Would it make it easier for you, Anna? You'd feel better if you thought I'd had one?"

"You're determined to be disappointed. It's how you live."

"I called about Alex, Anna."

"It's a mistake to tell you the truth."

"I may as well tell you—I look forward to these calls."

"You call."

"You're hard to get anything by, Anna."

"I have to go. I'm going. I should have lived on my own before Alex. It could have worked. I could have worked. We could have had Alex later. You would like me now. With Alex we rushed."

Rushed Alex ground me down. I installed double-key bolts in the outside doors so she couldn't get out at night. I left the storms up year-round. But if Alex wanted to be out, she just didn't come home. Or, locked in, she would break things. Alex home or not, I couldn't sleep. She refused all help, even when, at the professional's prompting, I offered cash. I had her forcibly admitted to

rehab, but she escaped. (There was a period during which she ref
ered to herself as *Genie*.) When at home, Alex took things, or sh
left things. The day she truly cleared out, she left a video of her
self having sex. She centered it on my bed: "You're in luck
Duck," she wrote, "these usually cost."

The week Alex turned eighteen, she demanded money and th
car. I'd just served dinner. We were sitting in the kitchen. I tol
her no. I told her as a driver she was not to be trusted. She threw
a fork at my head. I slapped her. She hurled her plate, then lef
the house, then drove off. As best as I can know, Alex stopped at
hill's crest in town near the college, set the transmission in Neu
tral, stepped out. Intentional or not, it was the sort of thing Ale
would do.

In its descent, the car bounced along a dozen parked one
bounced through an intersection, slammed into someone's home
In the morning paper, Hi-Country Towing was extracting my ca
from a house. In the photo, a couple stands on their porch, direc
sun in their eyes. The young mother holds a child. People coul
have died. When the police came by, I told them the car had bee
stolen, that I'd, alas, left the keys on the dash, in the door loc
something. "Not a criminal act," the younger cop said, though
couldn't quite read him.

Early on, I believed Alex more careless than destructive, thoug
what we decide to think about our children is meant to protect u
Alex, shall we say, *forgot* things. She used other people's thing
without asking. She *lost* things. The last winter she at lived hom
I bought her three coats. The same winter, one bitter night, sh
let her Brandy out and the cocker froze.

I had driven to Denver and a night blizzard had forced me to
motel. Because I'd called, I thought I'd arranged things. I pulle
in the next morning to a dog on the porch. Golden-haire
Brandy. I thought of corn stubble. Straw. I toed at Brandy's ribs.

"Christ Jesus, you couldn't let her in. Oh, Alex."

"Oh."

"She practically clawed through the door."

Children stay in your life, even from a good ways off. In th
service, I got sucker punched in the ring (a long-armed Michi
gan black), flattened after the bell. Sucker punched was how
felt when my daughter'd phone. She'd call, I'd answer, grip th

phone, speak: sound fully adult—*responsible, adept, unlucky*—then wake to gall pumping up the tube of my throat. Like a chemical spill, broken plumbing. I learned if I answered the phone to Alex to sit on the floor.

I was billed for an abortion. (Alex's note to me: *Call him*—she meant the doctor—*if you want, up to you*.) Unitemized, the charge felt struttingly inexact. But how would I have wanted the bill labeled: *Misfire? Benedictus? Dud?* And what *was* the procedure worth? I called Anna.

"Who would marry a person like that? All day snuffing babies?"

"Did you say snuffing, Anna?"

"Where's Alex?"

"What I got was the bill."

"Call the quack—*the son of a bitch*—I'll do it. If I had the number, I'd do it."

"If you had the number?"

"Don't teach me to be a mother—*I am one.* Now, have you talked to her? Did she call?"

"I've talked to her, Anna. I washed her underwear. I took her to the doctor and dentist. I drove to PTA. I bought Kotex. I talked to her."

Anna hung up before I did.

I dialed the number on the bill, a toll call to a college town upstate. The telephone was quickly picked up, but the voice, a woman's, was as paced as dawn. The voice informed that my daughter's address and phone were protected information. The voice called my daughter Sunny.

"That's right, s-u-n. Sun. Sunshine."

"Protected from what?"

The receptionist insisted I understood.

It felt as if I were talking to Anna. I tried for a picture of the woman. I said: "I'm here."

"Doctor's busy."

"I bet."

The receptionist punched me on hold.

I studied the bill—*Practice Limited to Abortion*: "*5 minutes from Thruway Exit 7*" actually printed beneath *Charles Gizzi-Lish, M.D.,* as if he were a mechanic with particular skills. Fuel injectors. Disc brakes.

Still on hold, if what I longed for was a feeling of bane or dis
gust, what I felt was fear, and a chromatic and knee-deep envy.
couldn't clear my brain of an Aquarium Pump in my own glove
hand—"*transforming a tedious and dirty job*"—sucking fish.

I switched hands with the phone. I was waiting for Gizzi-Lish
but when I heard a voice it was still the woman. She had pulle
Sunny's file.

I couldn't see the point of arguing names. "Sunny's of age."

The woman ticked off the confirmable fribble of my life—al
the numbers that applied. She read as though if she reported a
error she expected me to correct it. Then she wanted to confirm
my signed consent for all expense.

"Not mine."

"Notarized."

"Not mine. What sort of name is Gizzi-Lish anyhow?"

The woman hung up.

By the time I next saw Sunny, I had moved. I'd changed jobs
towns, and I'd not called Anna. I had an unadvertised phone an
address. But Sunny found me. I wasn't surprised. Sunny at my
door as night fell felt as logical as the cold tile under my feet tha
morning.

In the morning, a cold sun had glared, faking heat. By after
noon it had begun to snow, then had stopped. I'd just begun writ
ing ads again for extra income, this time for a motorists' club ou
of Jersey—Perth Amboy. *Over 60 Personal Safety Product.
Discounted Below Store Prices!* It was Saturday, and I'
worked part of the day. I'd done my best to enjoy myself, as thes
days I wrote the blurb ads before drinking:

The **De Luxe Self-Inflating Blood Pressure Monitor** (To
ranked by a leading consumer magazine! **Perfect for Travel**
Peace of Mind!)

Practice **CPR** *and other emergency life-saving procedures i
the comfort of your home.* **Convenience!** A life-size **mannequi**
(easy snap-together assembly) with a comprehensive 40-pag
study guide (color illustrations!). American Heart Associatio
approved. You'll learn CPR, mouth-to-mouth breathing, an

the Heimlich maneuver. **You'll know what to do!** Home CPR System . . . $69.95.

Reduce second-hand smoke with **SmokeSnatcher.** Quiet, space-age fan draws smoke into its unique charcoal filter! **As Seen on TV!**

Store your loaded gun in our **EZ-Access Vault.** Tamperproof! You can reach your weapon in a hurry with your private security code—**even in the dark!** Braille-like code buttons.

Telescoping Ice Scraper. Ideal for your truck, van, or car— stay clean and dry! No more risking an injuring slip on ice, or overstretching! **Only 100 Left!** Reduced . . . $12.95.

Don't commute without Safety Man—*a simulated male that appears fit and 6' tall. Of the highest quality inflatable vinyl construction,* **Safety Man** *weighs 8 lbs. Your bodyguard (and companion!)—whether you are at home alone or driving alone in your car. Designed as a one-of-a-kind visual deterrent, this believable security device looks real. Dress him in accordance with your personal style!* Can be deflated and stored or trans- ported in the optional tote bag. Can be ordered in skin tones of *creme, dusk, tan.* Repair patch included. Compare at $99.95. Our Price . . . $79.95. **You'll love Safety Man!**

Shatterproof Xmas Ornaments for a worry-free Holiday season! Includes six of each color in a set of 18. *Traditional*: red, green, gold. *Contemporary*: garnet, lapis, quartz. *New Wave*: as- paragasse, eggplante, yamme. And *New!*: gingerbread, cherry, meringue. **Protect your children and pets! HAPPY (and safe) HOLIDAYS!** Set of 18 . . . $19.95.

It had passed 4 P.M. and had darkened. It felt time for a drink. I cleared my desk, moved to the kitchen. I passed through my liv- ing room on the way to catch a look outside. Snow floured the roads. I knew there'd be more, and I hadn't bothered earlier to sweep my walks. I started to pour a drink, then stepped out the back door and circled the house to survey things. The sky looked gorged as a blood tick.

Back inside, I poured gin. Then, as if to mark that, the front bell rang. No one but strangers rang there. Out of scale with the rest of the house, the ruby door appeared, from the road, large enough to drive a car through, and people, rather than confront it, normally traipsed round back. The front bell re-rang. I stood a moment on my side of the door, then opened. In the light from my hall, Sunny's face had the look of artist-worked wood, a rendering of skull.

My roofed porch was free of snow, but I didn't step out. Sunny and I both held our space and ground, which seemed normal enough. What was odd was that Sunny stood dressed for summer. She was shoeless and coatless, no socks. Her shirt was soaked and she steamed in the cold. Her hair was in balls. She smelled like leaked things.

My chest swelled with air. I held all the air, felt it process, then released it, then stretched back to the switch for the outside lights which illuminated as well a flood lamp—a brightness which blared like sound and which trained on my face. The flood lamp, set up for and left since Christmas, forced my hands up, so I altered my angle, putting Sunny's face between me and the glare. Then I looked past her head to the street. Who did I think I was? a father checking on his daughter's ride? Through a trick of light and dark and cold and vapor, the car's own exhaust obscured it. Then I saw it: a wrecked green heap. I next traced Sunny's trail. Her bare feet had melted footprints all the way from the car.

I refused to move from my door as if it were what? the door of an underinsured motel and I a loyal employee gauging risk? I balled a fist and thumped on the door, its windowless planks. I searched for a role—*judge? thug? sworded angel?*—forced a look at my daughter, fixed my stance to again situate her head to block light. Sunny's face, backlit, kept the look of wood, though now put me more in mind of a butcher's block than of sculpture. Her eyes soaked into the surface of her face like stains, the violet of pulped things: grapes, steak.

I clamped my eyes until I saw merged purpled hues. *Aurora borealis*. Through closed lids, I pictured Sunny, made her face alert, though Sunny's face when I opened and focused beamed blank. What you learn about bewilderment, effort, fatigue, and retreat is bewilderment, effort, fatigue, and retreat. And what you learn about pain is how to return it. Or is it that an act of will and hostility can feel like freedom? Sunny leaned forward, pushing a boxer's dulled jaw towards me. I raised a balled fist. Was it then I clubbed the door?

The driver raised out of the car. His woolen headdress glowed over the roof. He shouted something. At that moment, the city street lamps flared on, and you could see the day's snowfall re-priming, spitting down. I looked from the street lamps back to the shouter, who had reentered the car. The car's inside dome glowed. Inside the car, the shouter's headdress shone phosphorescent, like coral or fish. There were other fish in there—a couple of blacks, a second white slumped in the front seat. The wrecked car was the color of polluted water.

It seems to me now that the car was damaged, though I can't quite honestly vouch it. But the taillights must have been broken, trunk crushed, exhaust rotted, a banged door roped shut. Though, I admit, I've dreamed the car: sunlit, hubcapped, *primo*.

Sunny, you should know, didn't turn from my porch not speaking. She pronged a finger against my chest: "You a genius, Bloodsuck? Yet?" My body and her finger shook, but in the end, we both stood like posts. We stood like new ghosts. We stood like a crowd listening to a public phone ring. It was as though we had, as a group, cornered something.

I suppose you could think it should have been otherwise, but it wasn't. The courses of our lives were set and would not turn upon a chant, or a joke, a vote, prayer, plea, quiz, a concealed life-altering revelation. I felt numbed, seakindly dulled against what? a *daughter-nation? colony? child?* How could have anyone, I thought, really loved her? Yet there were people in a car who called for her, and who, it proved, would not drive away without her. You had to say that.

Sunny spoke her words and we stood. Snow melted in her hair. Then Sunny followed out her own steps on the walk. She first made troughs instead of footprints. Then she corrected her step, began lifting her feet with a sweet precision, setting them as delicately down, obeying some new inner, or remembered, order "No," would interpret Sunny's mother if I were to relate to her this part of the story. "Her feet were cold for God's sake. Just stop."

Not that I intended to call Anna. Not that I intended to inform a soul. Sunny's coming and leaving was my affair.

I watched.

It didn't seem Sunny was traveling through the actual expanse of my actual front yard, but as though she were passing, unnudged, through time, through geography, through weather.

At the car, Sunny clambered over the passenger white male who, unable or unwilling to move, didn't. She cradled herself between the two inert whites. Only the blacks seemed awake. Then, as with a will of its own, the car door Sunny had scrambled through slammed shut. The driver floored the gas. The car shot out flames, fired off. If the air had been formed of glass, it would have cracked with veins. What I inhaled as the car roared away felt slivered.

I stood on my porch in the unhindered light and shuttered my eyes. I felt afraid to move. I breathed in and out despite what seemed the danger of it. I stood very still. One of the blacks, from the car's lighted inside, pressed against the car's rear glass, arms spread like wings, or like weapons he was used to using. I appraised him in the yellow light of that car's back window as a man cubed in dirty ice. I pictured the blacks (though I only saw each in the car, shoulders up), as colossal, like reigning cons in a prison movie. Without seeing their shoes, I knew the shorter whites wore boots. I knew they would fight with their feet. They were kickers.

I visioned the carload that drove off with my daughter, but couldn't see her in that dream, not even, as I could have expected, the back of her head. *I'd wanted her gone.* Which I knew like knew I'd wanted to feel helpless about her going. But helplessness has to be unearned. You have to do even less than only to want it.

I descended to an image of the car as a kind of gritty evaporation (somewhere, already, prancing dust?). The solid part—flesh, bone, blood and nerve roads—of my daughter was gone, and could ignore it. What I couldn't dismiss were her footprints, but they had begun to fill. As if it had been all day, for this moment, gathered, snow tumbled. Were the fatter flakes radioactive? Did they, at some frequency, clang like bells? I felt surrounded by fierce ash. Though I felt, too, I should tell you, the pushy life of my blood and of the heavens, the uncurbed forward drift, the sustaining tide beneath my skin and of what seemed to me the unbidden forward tide of stars and star clots, their moons and their tethered planets.

As if I had a plan, I pulled my front door shut, then grasped my own pulsing wrist, then stepped from under the roof of my porch, gazing up. I held my wrist and my stare through the snow for the clear bowl of heaven I knew to be covered. I stared back at the ground to make my way down my walk, stepping into the sink of my daughter's double prints. In light cast by the lamp at the end of the walk, Sunny's imprints had the look of plain graves. Against that, I felt the motion of my own blood coursing. My skin radiated heat, and I felt I detected the unresting hot run of the heavens, the dust-and-gas galaxy I made part of. Then it registered I'd locked myself out. I turned to dash for the door then stopped, halted by the thought that some of the stars I admired were dead, that light from far suns was *not* proof. I turned away from my house to wade in the uncurved light of one of my city's street lamps. Then, in a neighborhood where dogs were to be penned, a setter tore by. I called for him, but he barreled through my yard as if he had just been shot at.

The front door was locked. The back door was locked. The windows were locked. All the storms were installed, except for the upstairs bath. That storm I'd dropped from the window and not replaced. I hauled the ladder from the shed, erected it to the bathroom window. As I climbed, I tried to gaze up, but the snow hurtled down. Flakes like tusks.

I relied on my wrists to hoist me. Blood pulsed every time I applied my wrists on the metal rungs, and I waited each time for the surging. Then at the bathroom window, two stories up, I realized what I'd known but had forgotten—that if I pried the window or broke the glass, the space was too small to crawl through. I considered driving my hands through the single-pane glass just to warm them. I leaned against the house, fists stuffed under my arms. I shifted my weight to secure my footing. The ladder slid

on the patio brick, then caught. I waited to breathe, then exposed
my hands, fumbled my way down. Already snow capped my
tracks on the ground. I left the ladder propped, then completed
yet another circle around the house, stared in the windows, tried
the doors, then stood in my owned white yard. *All that I saw
was mine.*

The flood lamp, spike rammed in the lawn in early December,
shone on a wreath hung for Christmas on the door. I tried to
wrench the light up, but the earth and the spike felt welded. I
strained again; things popped in my back. My back felt of a piece.
Though I tried, and was willing to deal with the pain, I couldn't
straighten. As though my back were shell, I kneeled to reach the
electrical cord, tangled my hands in the wire then, rising, gave it
a rip, bellowing. For all the pull and the noise, the cord barely
broke the snow, then sank. Under the snow, the cord shuddered
like a taken fish line. I held fast to the line, traced it. What I
wanted to find was the socket where I'd plugged into the extension I had run through the cellar foundation through a hole I'd
bored with one of my father's old hand tools. But where the
socket should have been, the snow had crusted and I couldn't grub
through it. My fingers looked to me like birds' feet.

I rummaged between the shrubbery and my house, tramped
the snow. What I uncovered was an old croquet ball, which I
turned and fired at the Christmas flood lamp that illumined me. I
missed, wild right. I recovered the ball, then, kneeling before the
seal-beam lamp, used the ball to smash at the glass. But the glass
bore up, and I had to work. Because I faced the lamp, I only now
see the shadow of myself on the door. I worked on the lamp (long
after it had broken) until I sweat, then, still on my knees in the
snow, I rested. I'd managed to slice my palm. The back of my
shirt stiffened in twitches I could feel, then froze. Still I rested. I
crowded fingers into my mouth, then rose with the ball, spun
threw. I shattered an upstairs window, though only the storm.

I looked down the street for Milo's. I knew he lived in my old
town, but I looked anyway. My feet ached. My hands shook.
Snow was down my neck, on my head. My shoulders were white.
The hair skirting my neck was frozen.

Still, my senses were not altogether blunted by the exposure. I
felt in a way, in fact, stirred, and if, for only an instant, back on the

ridge in Colorado with my daughter, tramping home. Together we diverged from the packed tracks of the fire road to Alex's path through the fixed black trees of the forest in snow still refusing to cave beneath her. Walking atop that snow (its support a swaggering grace), wearing my red wool cap, she was as tall as I.

When I think of my daughter now, I think of how diminished she looked on my porch: the shirt—a man's—is unstrained against her breasts. She seems resolutely undeveloped. I see her shirtsleeves turned above her wrists, her cuffs above her knees. Did she think she was approaching warm seas, or had she just missed a season? However had she found me? Had she thought she was home? Had I been expected to answer her query? Of course, I could have: "*Genius*? Hardly, Alexandra. No." But to not confuse you: I didn't trap the girl on my porch, haul her in, or weep, or curse, or shout after her car. I was not without choices. Of course not.

Fathers

His daughter, Alex, is named for a lead in a sixties movie in which the title role is a lying blonde—*Alexandra*—a kleptomaniac and adulterous woman. Late this birthday, Alex, tonight thirteen, wants facts: "*Tell* me again," she calls from her bed. She has tried to contact her mother tonight, by phone. He, the father, snugs her in. "Kleptos are thieves. They steal." Then: "Alex, in the movie, was beautiful. You too."

"You named me Alex."

"I named you Alexandra."

Alex, who has never seen the movie which stars her name, has begun lately to act as if she has. When she questions her father about that Alex, she pretends she's reminding herself of things she and her father both know.

In the movie, the father unintentionally recalls, a senescent nun educates her Alexandra: *If you lie, you'll cheat, if you cheat, you'll steal. Don't start in now by spinning me stories.* The same nun also warns Alex not to bathe in her father's or brother's tub water, further charging Alex to *situate*—the nun's distinct, whispered word—a thick book between her and a male should Alex, by foreseen terrible chance, be forced to sit on a boy's or man's lap. The old nun positions young Alex's face between her hands, peers in. That Alex's face seems to this father, in recollection, sapped, frightened, a face that looks robbed.

"Alexandra," he says.

Alex lifts her eyes at what seems to him—even him, the Adam of this small race, *this nation*—the sudden strange sound of her name.

The
Peacock
Throne

---

*Shah Muhammad Reza Pahlavi's father, Reza
Khan, is an iron man. Reza Khan*—King of Kings, Shadow of the
Almighty, Light of the Aryans, God's Vicar, Center of the Universe, *and* Commander in Chief—*builds roads, railways, airports, factories, schools, banks. His army herds nomads to the
cities, levels mosques, imprisons or murders priests (the mullahs), strips women in the streets. Crowds are thinned and dis-
persed with bullets. The army is well fed. People disappear.*

*Shah Muhammad Reza Pahlavi inherits his father's generals,
but not his father's height. Reza Pahlavi, early, sports elevator
shoes, orders slaughters from the palace. The generals kneel before the son, kiss the shoes. In a land of flowing oil, Pahlavi's sub-*

jects collect cow dung to dry for fuel. Pahlavi's first wife, Fawzia, bathes daily in sweetened milk.

Reza Pahlavi, new Lord of Energy to the West, erects monuments of himself, vows creation of a second America founded on petroleum, poly-religion, concrete, plastic. Reza Pahlavi stands for photo ops for reporters. In public, he models European suits. On some level, based on these photos and selected quotes, the West forwards enthusiastic bribes, advisors, guns. A King's vanity, we learn, is different from our own. He has, among his king things, an armed army at hand.

In his turn, Reza Pahlavi releases his army into the streets. The army is well fed. Hooded students, in European airports, pass pamphlets to hurried crowds. In Paris, at Orly Airport, a group of students remove their shirts, their shoes. They display flayed backs, charred toes. One has no eyelids. (Were you to ask, he might explain he'd clamped his eyes against the torture of friends and that his closed lids had been burned away with lighted cigarettes.) At night, the students hobble to gather pamphlets from Orly's floors.

In Persia, death is followed by forty days of mourning. It is believed that on the fortieth day mourners can pronounce the names of killers, and that at that moment of pronouncement murderers will shudder in their shoes. "Death to the Shah" becomes the rhythm of Iran at intervals of forty days.

Shah Muhammad Reza Pahlavi weeps when he flees Teheran. He explains to the Western press he has less money than people think. From the Shah's residence in Saint Moritz, a courtier points, for French TV, to a photo in an old copy of Paris-Match. The photo is a close-up of the Shah's second infertile queen, Soraya Esfandiari, who in a lift line with others waits, democratically, to ski.

The expelled Reza Pahlavi roams, searches for a home. In disbelief, he dies barefooted in an unowned bed. For the news, the thin-boned Farah, the last of Pahlavi's wives, stands in Egypt, regally facing east, the whirring cameras. Her eyes crouch.

The state funeral in Cairo is almost private. Lionheartedly, Sadat welcomes two haggard kings, Nixon and Constantine of Greece. The three of them bury the Shah. Shortly, it is noted, rich Persians pop up in France and Beverly Hills.

Meantime, Islamic holy men squabble in medieval Persian streets eyeing house-sized portraits of The Awaited One— Khomeini—he who disappeared in the ninth century to now return to deliver his faithful from misery and the trod of kings. Afterward comes the End of the World. In evidence, royal tanks park in streets, untended. Crowds gather and part at will. Loudspeakers sprout like plants. Women dress from head to foot. But then: in Qom, Teheran, Tabriz, Meshed, Isfahan—under the hand of the Charitable and Merciful One—people begin to disappear.

Before Maryam, I judged Pahlavi and Khomeini on the denominator of tyranny and murder alone. When factions permit themselves excess, do you compare immediately the visions and end intentions of the regimes? Or do you, like me, first stack and count the bodies? I start with bodies because counting feels concrete, and because it takes me time to think the unthinkable. Like anyone, I'd hoped the Islamic revival would have ended the corruptions and deaths attending the Shah's wish to purchase a modern civilization, but under the Khomeini, secret trials and murders increased. I next hoped for some virtuous differences in the killings, but it was no go. If as a child I wished hard for the ability to know, at will, the thoughts in people's heads, as an adult, I've not harbored the wish for years.

My attention to world affairs is, I suppose, both as serious and fitful as yours, but the affairs in Iran were impossible to ignore: the bodies, the bodies. I avoided as best I could thinking about the reasons. Maryam bought me time. I could think of Iran as Maryam. You might have guessed she possessed the kind of beauty that, if allowed, would make you gasp. And she announced she was the daughter of the dead Shah. She called Shah Muhammad Reza Pahlavi her illegitimate sire.

I corrected the idiom of her English. "You are the illegitimate *child*."

"He was my *illegitimate* sire. He gave my mother me. If he had produced a son, he would have married her, owned me. He married Farah for sons. He sent my mother, my sisters, and me to Paris, then here." Her hand swept west. "He sent us to live in Kentucky."

Do I know if Muhammad Reza Pahlavi fathered Maryam?

I know, for two days in 1983, I came to believe I was with a princess. Of course, I wanted to believe. What would you have done if a pretty woman told you her dead father was a king?

Two weeks before Christmas, I'm visiting Washington, D.C. A wet raw day, storm brewing. Even now, I breathe in the day's smell of unfired clay. By contrast, the East Building of the National Gallery of Art appeared bathed in drier light. White rising stone, white sharpened stone. I thought, at that moment, of sand. Beaches in Algiers. I thought of Camus's stranger, the sad Meursault, who murders the Arab, firing and firing the unowned gun. Questioned, Meursault comments on the weather: "The sun was hot." Are we to believe the murder Meursault commits is an act brought on only by the blurring of the conscience by something as unsought as midday weather? Afraid we were, and thinking of worldwide torture and murder committed in the name of God and might, I backed into the street, peered up again at I. M. Pei's uncowardly construction—a *higher* church than the city's Pentagon or National Cathedral, stone havens, both, of fear and control and the harvesting force to back it. Cold beaded the air. The trees on the grounds looked bony. A four o'clock sun. The sky, dim, seemed backlit by sullen technicians. Ieoh Ming Pei's milled granite shone.

I shoved the museum's revolving door. The flaps on the door scraped hard. The guards at the door both frowned. I asked directions to a restroom. One of the guards pointed the way. The other, with his thumb, mashed me into his handheld counter.

I washed my face, then my hands, then drank from them cupped. The restroom smelled dry. I skipped the escalator, hiked the stairs. My shoes sounded on the marble. Calder's overfed mobile twisted, bloody red, stirring air. At the top of the stairs and in the open, I was the lone tourist. I looked down at the guards. Outside, I could see snow falling.

I moved towards noise. In the first gallery an old woman shouted at an older man in a foreign tongue. The man settled his palm on her sternum, pushed away, an old skiff from a dock. The woman began to weep.

In the next gallery, Maryam was alone. Cross-legged on the floor, she propped a sketching pad against herself, beneath her breasts. She copied a street scene by Manet, though the museum caption protectively complained: *attributed inconclusively*.

Maryam adjusted her pose. Twin bracelets spun on a wrist. Maryam wore army pants with the pant legs rolled above dark socks. Her teeth were straight. She wore rough-out, soft-soled boots. The sweater nubby.

The sketch was of an execution: a half-dozen French or Prussian soldiers, arms awry—musket ball and flesh—common men forever dying, in Manet's oil, and, now, in Maryam's lead.

Maryam rose, frowned at the finished work. In retrospect, she seems a rouseable Persian from, say, fifty, seventy years before, complete but for horse and carbine. Reza Khan's Palace Guard. She opened her mouth to her teeth, strode to me: "To see not the power of another culture is to prepare to perish from ignorance—as democracies will."

"Whoa, what's that?" I put up my hands.

Maryam pronounced her name, then threaded her arms into an embroidered vest, shrugged up her sweatered shoulders, shook her head. Her breasts rolled beneath the wool. A David Lean production: horses and rifles. Sand. Fruited palms. Outcroppings. In the midst of the crowd, the camera selects, zooms. Dark marble eyes, lightless and alert.

Maryam was sleeping, she said, in Georgetown.

When we stepped outside to night, I buttoned my coat, hailed a cab. On leave from the University of Kentucky, Maryam had traveled first to New York to see friends, then to D.C. to sketch federal buildings. She found, she said, she disliked most of the city's structures. From the cab, she pointed at a columned building. "This work is little risk. I trust but Saarinen." Because I knew, I asked if he were the architect famous for designing airports. Disappointed, Maryam ticked off a list of Eero Saarinen jewels: the Hockey Rink at Yale; the chapel at MIT; CBS in New York; *yes,* the Dulles Airport twenty miles away, and TWA in New York; but the St. Louis Arch too; and chairs. "You know the chairs?"

"I don't know."

"You can tell his mother was a sculptor." She seemed sad. For Maryam, the deceased émigré, Saarinen, was her United States. In this way—the national embrace of a foreign artist—she had managed to forgive, as deeply as she could, U.S. betrayal of her Iran.

"Betrayal?" I said, though I knew, in detail, of the U.S.-backed ousting of Mussadegh, the Iranian premier who, for a couple of years in the fifties, had managed to nationalize Iranian oil. The U.S. had bolstered a gluttonous monarchy against a nation's masses, and stood fast for SAVAK, the Shah's secret police, whose primary methods of torture involved electricity and flame, with some reliance on simple beatings. But which betrayal did Maryam mean? Given the alleged parentage, had she expected more—or less?—support for the Shah from the U.S.? Maryam stared at me. I didn't press. I accepted that a dead Finn's lyrical anchorless forms, dotting the East Coast and Midwest, allowed me room in a cab with a princess. Maryam quizzed me about my airport. She wanted me to have arrived at Dulles. She wanted, she said, to talk about Saarinen's use of cables to support large roofs while providing surprising column-less space. I told her I'd arrived at National, which was true.

I paid for the taxi. I would have anyway, but Maryam didn't seem to have a cent. In the short ride in the cab, she scolded me for my ignorance of her Saarinen: *He is joy! He is joy!* She spoke, too, of the Shah, her own accused dead father, her own accused dead king.

What is needed for revolution, I paused to instruct myself, is an awareness of poverty and oppression. And, beyond that, an awareness that these conditions are *not* the natural order of this world. It is unrighteous authority that provokes revolution, but as in the case of the Khomeini, a revolution can demolish so fully that it annihilates the very ideals which served as germ. Then again, I thought, the principle of revenge is simple, long-lived, and older than mind. I stopped the thinking, turned back to the bloom of my queen.

We found a bar. Maryam designated a Dr Pepper. Considering the weather, I considered bourbon, then ordered gin.

I asked Maryam what she thought of Pei's building, the museum. She said the triangular motif was obsessive. "It's everywhere—*partout*," she said in French—"columns, ceilings, tiles, stairs, even doorframes." Then: "Building tools are constructed for rectangles. Pei's building is ego, ego, ego. It was, I think, for builders, chaos." Then: "A building sliced to shape by a knife for bread."

"A sharp knife," I suggested.

It was after Maryam's murder that I learned that, of the two dissenting votes by the six-member Washington Commission of Fine Arts for Pei's building, one had been cast by Saarinen's widow, Aline.

---

plastic explosive, noun
A versatile explosive substance in the form of a moldable doughlike solid, used in bombs detonated by fuse or electrical impulse (e.g., doorbell, auto ignition). Also termed *plastique*.

I circled the gallery twice. She sat before, as I've said, a street scene by Manet; that is, a scene "attributed" to Manet. Still, the painting had been painted and would have pulled despite its questioned stock. I paused beside Maryam's right shoulder.

Her blackberry hair, massed to one side, struck as clean, loose goods, splendid cargo which she masked with a Basque beret. Her pants, army green, were baggy—a fit woman in fat pants—and rolled above socks and rough-out boots. Her sketching hand was clean, but the thumb of the left, pressing the pad beneath her breasts, was smudged. A heavy knit, her sweater hung creamy, in folds and piracy, lapping its high collar about her neck. Twin bracelets chimed on her wrist.

When she looked at me, I felt measured.

The paintings on the walls excused us to walk, and we walked, and had soon agreed on a drink in Georgetown. It was where she was, she said, residing at present. On leave from architectural studies in Kentucky, she complained about her professors, whose talents she suspected. "Even as a child in Teheran, I read books I bring myself to school. I hold them on my legs while the mistress speaks. Later I hold them high. When I am very young, I read your country's books."

"In English?"

"Sometimes English."

There would have been conversation.

Maryam: "I spent time in New York—at Columbia—with friends."

I knew the Shah had been admitted to the seventeenth floor (the entire floor) of the Cornell Medical School in New York. "Did you see him?"

"I was seen by agents. I fled with my friend on her motorbike."

"Agents?—your father's? Khomeini's?"

"My father is my father, and he was ill."

"The Shah's presence here wasn't medical—it was political."

"You told this to his tumors?"

"Henry Kissinger, Frank Sinatra, Tricia Nixon Cox visited him. You couldn't get in?" Had the conversation occurred, we would have been talking about three-year-old history.

"I'd come to stay with a friend—I wanted to at least see the hospital. The street was filled with protesters calling for the Shah's death. They might not recognize Frank Sinatra, but there are certain who know me, who had been waiting their day."

"Being king is a supremely privileged human condition. Anger against the Shah had some ground in fact and repression— enlightened anger."

"More enlightened than—what?—*We're going to ship you back, and you're not going to like it. No more booze. No more Big Macs. No more rock music. No more television. No more sex. You're going to get on that plane at Kennedy, and when you get off in Teheran, you're going to be back in the thirteenth century. How you gonna like that!*"

"Where was this?"

"Columbia." Then: "After the embassy seizure, I made a point of walking with friends. Women. I felt safer. American men have always been willing to fight foreign men."

I made a point of the irony that Khomeini had, early on, sought and received political asylum in the West. "For him to have instigated the invasion of an embassy violates a principle of diplomatic immunity that even the most rogue governments have professed to respect."

"Fancy talk from a citizen of a country whose educated come up with giant posters of John Wayne and American flags and *We're going to kick your butts!* Most Iranians in the U.S. had a father or brother or mother killed by the Shah, but not all of them are satisfied with Khomeini's revolution."

I said I supposed you could no more vicariously live wealth than you can poverty or subservience. "But you're sounding fair about it—I'll say that."

"All Iranians here are harassed in some way or other by outriders of SAVAK or outriders for the mullahs, and, now, outriders for the U.S. Most Iranians of any mind have said something that would incense some side and put themselves at risk."

"On whose side do you vote? The Shah's? Of course."

"I have many reasons to be unhappy with my father, Shah Reza. But I am alive—so. We are born to our lives. We cannot avoid our lives. And Grandfather loved me," Maryam said. "He held me when I was small. In his large arms, he possessed me." Then: "Think otherwise if you must, but most loyalties are instinctive, an accident of circumstance, or both. Loyalties are not so easily a matter of choice." Maryam launched into French— "There must be, of course, capacity for doubt and regret, but my family held me in their arms."

Then, English: "For your country I worry for this impression of helplessness. Perception of impotence may provoke other probes of your nation's will. Wild as the mullahs might be, they would never touch the Soviet Embassy or, ever, the Israelis. See?"

I said: "The National Iranian Oil Company is selling seven hundred thousand barrels of oil a day to the U.S. During the Shah's heyday it was only nine hundred thousand."

"The same week my father died, the Khomeini ended whatever pretense there might have been about Islamic tolerance. *We want*

Islam alone! Nothing but Islam! he shouted. Twenty prisoners were marched out of the Evin Jail. The guards fired enough to kill these men many times, but they continued. Prison officials chanted *Allahu Akbar! God Is Great!* People are executed in Teheran," Maryam said. "For civil crime."

Maryam produced a series of photographs of four prisoners. Heads hooded, they were buried chest deep in sand. The presiding judge cast the first stone, then five others joined in selecting and throwing from a pile of apple-sized rocks. The hooded men and women had been accused of promiscuous sex. "It takes fifteen minutes of stoning to kill people."

"You make it sound like biology class or something—an experiment."

"Experiment? When the sentence of death is pronounced in Iran, it is carried out." Then: "When Carter sends his eighty thousand-ton *Kitty Hawk* towards Iran, he should understand martyrdom is an honor."

"Jimmy sends warships and Bibles to the Gulf and, you're right, he believes he's armed, but it's not just the U.S. and Iran—it's the Crusades turned round. Arabs versus Infidels. But maybe better Carter than Nixon? Nixon wrote to your father he envied the way he dealt with dissidents."

"A series of presidents, going back to Roosevelt—especially Nixon—armed my father to his teeth, encouraged him, sucked at cheap oil, sold him planes."

It was hard not to hear Reagan, as I had on TV, criticizing Carter. *The Shah might still be in power had Carter followed a consistent policy that we should have for a country that has been a strong ally and friend.*

Maryam: "When people believe their destination is preordained—you should listen now, I'm going to lecture—they will not have much faith in temporal arrangements or their ability to manipulate events. Islam teaches all is transitory—*nothing is permanent*—the only reality being death and the hereafter. The future can be neither known nor trusted. For an intensely religious Muslim, safety is a dangerous illusion. The odd upshot of all this is that Iranians are exaggeratedly preoccupied with self-preservation and self-interest. Except for soccer there are no team sports in Iran. There is a glorification of the individual in Iran that Americans are unaware of. They'll be a long and dangerous enemy. Put another way, underlying Iran is a strong sense of self-preservation and a bias toward anarchy. Hardly a stable combination in times of war or peace. America should learn to deal with nations and peoples as they are, not as they wish them to be. In the great game of world politics, you should abide by the ancient rule of having no permanent friends or enemies, only permanent interests. And this too: revolution and change through revolution seem more permanent and lasting features of the human condition than many others." Then: "It was taking the Shah in that goaded the mob to storm the embassy and take hostages."

"The Shah died in a Cairo hospital."

"It may have been why Sadat was murdered."

"Islamic purity? The whole atmosphere is blood. Murder politics."

"Three years ago, right after my father's death, Tabatabai, a spokesman for the Shah at the Iranian Embassy, had been bold in his opposing the Revolution. He was called to the door in his home here—in Bethesda. A man wearing a postal uniform asked him to sign for a special delivery, then pumped bullets after bullets into Tabatabai's stomach, then drove away in a U.S. postal jeep."

"There are more university students from Iran than from any other foreign country. And they're lucky to be students in the U.S. where they can take advantage of their visas to picket against the U.S.—OK? Where else can you march—unarmed—with banners like DEATH TO AMERICA IS A BEAUTIFUL THING"?

"Remember what they wrote in France of the rescue disaster. Really, what can you think of the effectiveness of a military on which a good half of the planet depends which is not capable of safely putting down two planes in the desert? In a night desert area, the planners forgot about dark and sand?"

Surely Maryam would have guessed I knew of the ground collision in which eight U.S. soldiers died outside Teheran. The fueled plane and helicopter nearly melted in the fire. "It was a plane and a helicopter, Maryam." Then: "Was your father so blind to the needs and values of his people that he resorted to enough repression that they finally turned? The consequences of his blindness threaten to be more terrible than the worst excesses of his regime. He's dead, but he's managed to be wrong twice."

"My father wrote of *his* father—the Reza Khan—'Strong men trembled just to look at him.'" Then: "My father wore elevator shoes." Then: "There is much falseness. Teheran, with its Tokyo traffic, has no sewer system. I know all these." Then: "He formed a toothless parliament. He ran the country for profit. Even the middle class, grown by industrialization and education, revolted because of lack of political rights, the centralizing of power, and a system in which top jobs were awarded based on only loyalty. I know all these." Then: "You would have me what—be born a boy?"

I would have told Maryam I was sorry for the baiting.

"I too. Of course, I follow my father's life. I know he set up SAVAK."

I would have admitted what I knew too: "With the cordial assistance of the CIA."

"When my father was asked if he knew of SAVAK torture, he said, 'We don't need to torture anymore.' An odd admission, no?"

"Is it a surprise people hate corruption and police terror?"

Maryam said she had at least one hundred blood relatives in the U.S. She pointed to the ailing matriarch of the House of Pahlavi, Queen Mother Tajomolouk. "Iranian students stoned her estate in Beverly Hills, but I believe she was in Paris. She does her serious shopping in Paris." Then: "If I am common Iranian, then what I think I think is this: If I oppose before the government, I am told I oppose the Shah. Now I am told I oppose God. It is not the same? It is all the same."

In the Georgetown bar, the jazz drives willfully, and Maryam is nearly impossible to hear, but as if in compensation, the lights dim, and the table candles reflect flame off skin. I feel honest and accurate and drink my fifth gin. Maryam works on her second Dr Pepper. When the trio completes its set and takes a break, Maryam lays colored pencils in a row, selects four, then five, then clears a space.

Two women are brought and seated beside us. Maryam and I are asked to shift our chairs. The younger of the two new women is pregnant.

"You may move your face," Maryam says to me, "but you must look at my direction."

I order another drink. Hadn't harems been renewed in the retracting Iran? Maryam's breasts tremble with the quick movements of her hand. Ancient wars for soil. Loam. I stare into the agate of her eyes. Maryam resets my right hand on my left arm.

The pregnant woman removes her fur. She's drinking beer.

"You're drinking?" The women have been conversing, but hear me and stop. I grin enough to show my teeth: we share a common language. I return to Maryam. She is working, but drawing mostly watching me, not the pad. The two women resume their conversation. I turn back. They stop. The pregnant woman taps her chest. "Me?"

"Should you be drinking?"

"A little. Sure."

"If it's a girl, what will you name it?"

"It?"

"Her."

She scrapes her chair closer to Maryam, who raises the pad for her to see.

"Yes?" says Maryam.

The woman nods.

Maryam displays a blunted pencil. "I have much love for gray."

The pregnant woman takes the pencil to the bar, has it sharpened. She returns with a beer.

My women.

As she draws, Maryam keeps licking her thumb. "The skirt falls," she says, shows me, then rubs the thumb on the pad where color and line are blooming. I detect ears, a neck.

The women rise to leave. "Hold it," I say, then ask Maryam to sign her name. Maryam selects a sharp black pencil, signs her name in Farsi: two vertical, looping lines. Two lines. A spare beauty, which, without exaggeration, at that moment, induces for me the tenderness of temporary immunity from the danger of life.

"Here," I pronounce to the coming mother, "name her *this.*" She stands in place, elbows propped on her stomach.

"It's *Maryam.*" I touch the paper, then the side of Maryam's face. I feel bilingual. The woman puts the paper in her purse, then her mother helps her with the fur.

"You drink beer when you carried her?"

"Some," the older woman admits. "Sure."

The waitress cleans the women's table, asks if I want a drink. I look at Maryam. "What does it mean?"

"It is a flower in Iran. Me as flower. I."

"Draw it?"

Instead, Maryam turns her pad for me to see. The drawing had looked more like me to me from upside down and across the table. Still, it *is* me. In line and blot. Wounds of navy, lavender, black, red, gray. Maryam had begun the rendering of the left lens of my prescription glasses, but had abandoned the full fact of my fixed vision. I point and raise my brows.

"I draw the part for as long as I find interest."

———

Past midnight, I'm walking Maryam to a house in Georgetown, a wide row brownstone, three floors and steps scraped of ice and salted. We'd walked blocks in the wrong direction until I asked and we faced about. Before we retraced, Maryam tightened the scarf at my neck. "I know it is wrong direction, but I am happy."

I fingered her face again.

"Yes?" she said.

Maryam had a key, yet it felt unclear to me why she was staying here—*how* she was staying here—in *this* neighborhood. She seemed penniless. I expected to see Henry Kissinger's dog or something. Bob Woodward. J. Edgar's replacement. *Someone.* I thought of Maryam's claimed, dead father, and looked about for guards. It registered I was in no condition to fight or run.

"I do not invite you in. This is not a terrible thing? Yes?"

I grip her elbow. "May I kiss you? May we kiss?"

"For sure," she says, her English leaping forward.

I kiss her, then step away, the dark morning wet and chill, halos smoky about the street lamps. A groomed and collared cat crouches in the corner of the steps of the residence of Henri Poussin, M.D. Maryam waits for me to pull away further before she tries her key, then pushes the bell.

SAVAK, a contraction of Farsi words for security and information organization. Following the ascension of the Islamic republic, a SAVAK official appears on Western TV. On screen, the official's face is distorted, voice warped: "Many of us will have problems making ends meet."

Or I could say that on the following day, I returned to the Georgetown jazz pub, that Maryam was sitting at our table, that she'd brought vials of colored ink. When the waitress took my order, Maryam asked for a glass of water for her pens.

Did I buy her dinner and fruit juice? Did I walk her to her house again to say goodbye? Had she forgotten her key and have to shout "Louie! Louie!" from the sidewalk, pressing the bell?

Or do I say—all praise be to Allah!—on my final night in D.C., I walked Maryam to my hotel where, with neither appeal nor constraint, this woman-child-woman transported me with Islamic soldiery and grace, her tongue trilling in derision, possession, pleasure? Rifles and shouts. Uneroded Euphratean soil "Five times a day I used to pray," says Maryam, astride me, facing east. "You have slept with many men?" I ask, falling into her syntax and inflection. Her answer is no and someplace between innocence and conviction.

Or, that arriving at the brownstone, late for a second night, that her sleeping bag and pack are propped against the doorframe. Does she say, "Louie took my key. He was displeased with my late hours"? I invite Maryam to my hotel, but is it she or I who arranges the couch into a second bed?

Think of it this way: We move from Georgetown toward the city.

Maryam: "Do you know the tale of the boy and the root?"

I adjust my scarf, rehitch her pack to my right shoulder.

"A boy comes upon a root held deep in the ground. He tugs, but the earth will not release. He is hungry, so he yanks. He yanks and yanks, then walks away. 'It matters hardly,' he shouts." Maryam clasps her sleeping bag and wicker box of crayons.

"That's it? The story's over? It seems to me it matters. The boy was hungry. Christ."

"You make sense of it, if you can shout, 'It doesn't matter.'" Maryam turns to face the night, talks to it.

We hike from Georgetown to Constitution, a good haul. The White House Christmas Tree is lighted, circled by more than fifty smaller pines, one for each of the voted-in states and all other possessions. Cars pass, whining in icy streets, and dark men squat on steel-grated heat ducts near the curbs of government buildings.

Overhead, as black as the black sky, an unseen flock of geese passes, their cries those of bafflement or hunger. Maryam scans blank air. "Poor, poor birds."

In time, we gaze upon the Washington Monument, all 555 feet and 5 ⅛ lighted inches of it. A razor moon emerges from cloud.

Maryam: "This monument is unkind."

Because what I see makes me think about it, I bring up Mount Saint Helens, the active volcano in Washington state. Dormant for more than one hundred years, it had two months before Reza Pahlavi's death erupted to kill sixty people and to jet a plume sixty *thousand* feet into the sky, to trigger fire and mudslide, to savage with ash. "Thirteen hundred feet of mountaintop disappear."

Maryam: "To reappear elsewhere."

"Just you wait, they'll turn a topped mountain into a national pearl. *Two* Washington monuments."

Maryam: "You are drunk." Then: "You rename what you're afraid of." She juts her chin at the memento before us. "So unkind."

At my hotel, Maryam asks for toothpaste, then enters the bathroom with only it. She emerges, face and teeth scrubbed? In the bathroom, the towel she's used lies folded on the sink, the small bar of hotel soap still wrapped but broken into.

I change my clothes for bed in the bathroom with the door shut. Before entering the bedroom I feel very nearly ashamed. But of what? the presence of royalty traveling light? a princess without a toothbrush?

Maryam is in her constructed bed. Beneath her blanket, I sense she is fully clothed. I crawl into my bed. All night I hear her tossing, bracelets chiming.

Within the year, twelve-year-old Iranians fling themselve against barbed wire or march, unarmed, into Iraqi mine fields i the face of machine-gun fire. The weaponless boys' ticket to par adise is a blood red headband and a small metal key they wea into battle. The headbands are stenciled in Farsi: "Sar Allah." S identified as divinely designated martyrs, the male children in tend to use their keys to enter directly into heaven if killed in th holy war against Iraq. Rounded up by the clergy, indoctrinate in the Shiite tradition of martyrdom, and bowing to the Ayatolla Ruhollah Khomeini's will, the backs of their khaki-colored shir declare: "I have the special permission of the Imam to ente heaven." As members of human-wave assaults, tens of thousand of such children have died. For the purpose of assured salvatior few pass puberty. An officer explains: "We have so few tanks."

The End of Times

A chum in high school: J, short for James, drove an Indian cycle he'd restored and christened *Judas*, blew sensible sax in the senior jazz band (the *Falconaires*); spoke in Pentecostal tongues. J wrote things in his school books like *The Desolation of Abomination.* Or:

The first angel sounded, and there followed hail and fire mingled with blood, and they were cast upon the earth: and the third part of the trees was burnt up, and all green grass.

J flew off the road near Butte, into lodgepole pines at a hundred miles per hour. He'd doused his bike and leggings in gas, struck a match, then raced down the road, then off it. The crash, visible from town, burned trees.

The school yearbook and the spring Senior Prom were dedicated to James.

There'd been one other candidate, Patti K, who'd been murdered following the Winter Formal, at which she'd been elected *Sno-Queen*. She and Harv Guld (our best trackman and *Falcon Athlete of the Year!*) had gone to park near Homestake Lake. They'd been drinking. By the time he was done, Harv'd strung up Patti like a doe and gutted her with a broken bottle, stuffed her into a new steel culvert. In time, Harv led police to Patti and to the picnic table he'd stood on to reach the limb with the rope. When the police asked why, Harv said, "Why? She threw up in my car. Why?"

Barrie (cont.)

Barrie selects a church, seats herself on the steps that rise to the pulpit, raises a French horn to her lips. Behind her the altar is draped, but bare.

During Barrie's long breaths, I hear shoes scrape on stone steps from the basement. An old priest peers in, sits beside me. The hand he raises in greeting has the look of stripped oak. He and I are seated in the back row of pews, from where his sighs are often as loud as the notes from Barrie. The old priest's right hand seeks his left as though it—knuckles and joints—were rosary. He pauses at each bump and hollow, rolls away dead skin with his thumb and finger.

The pews are hard dark wood and seem, most naturally, to impart a sentiment of intransigence and accusation. I sense what I can best describe as a thrill of unfitness. If my claim is I don't believe, why do I feel in the presence of this priest in this unlocked church irresolute and shamed?

Barrie: "I used to play this piece in my room in New Rochelle." There is a catch in her voice.

The priest, just then looking up, nods his head of hair. You, too, would wonder at this hair—its unexpected dirty strength, its taunt of multiplying cells. The priest tacks to the pew ahead to lift. I hear him on the steps again. It comes to me that the priest is deaf. It is something I know like I know Barrie's concert in this church is some form of unheard confession.

Stained glass, pitched just beneath the eaves, communicates a surrounding view of sky—strips of color—which in the startle of a dawn would urge upon a supplicant the impression of a miraculous and natant roof. *Jesus wants me for a sunbeam*—a child's melody coming home after thirty years, tripped by the imagined sights of morning prayer in this particular church—a church in which to pray, if you pray, eyes wide. *To shine for Him each day.* But the hour is dusk and the bar of westerly sun is dimming. Of a sudden, bright electric light scalds the chapel. I assume the bath of light has been offered as a gift from beneath, a bestowal. But Barrie interprets the light as interrogation, packs the horn.

Outside the church is an unlighted courtyard enclosed by yews, mulberries. Barrie and I sit on a weathered pew bolted to cracked stone. You live long enough to stop guessing the sentiments of another's human heart, but the entire scene—the untended trees, the broken paving, Barrie's face, the cased horn, the squamous pew—advances with such force of grief I can't imagine anyone's feelings being other than my own.

The night blackens, and the light from within the church, slowly and unforced, ribbons and lifts the roof. *A sunbeam*, though I sang it *sun-bean* as a child, unknowing, just as loud as I could. *I was a sun-bean for Him.*

First Barrie agrees to dinner, then says no. "Don't mind me, OK?" She asks me to flag a taxi. At the cab, she starts to kiss me, then turns toward the church. Floating on glass and light, the roof looks like a hat. Barrie says that. Then: "I adored the priest's hair. You *did*, right?"

In that dark, Barrie's closed eyes looked sealed. When I think of Barrie I see her in the streamlined church where she took me, three blocks from Capitol Hill. Of course, I see also the priest who, pulverulent or not, has outlived her. But there is this too: I hear song. I see colored light. I imagine dawn from inside Barrie's chapel. I keep her. *Barrie*. New, off center, self-shaped, alert. *The unexpected woman*. If it's true I look for them, then it's as true I'm off guard at each occurrence—persistently, terribly amazed—always, oh, always, amazed.

When I call, Barrie tells me she has somewhere to be by seven, but that I can accompany, that she'll drive. Her car is an American sedan—an old Dart—salt rusted from seacoast winters. She has to clear out the passenger seat for me. She tosses everything to the back, then gets out for me to slide in under the wheel. There's no door handle, inside or out, on the passenger side. The back seat of the Dart is littered with sheets of music and what looks to be weeks of unopened mail.

Everyone in, she sails into traffic. She lights a cigarette, passes it to me. I wave her off. She takes an expert drag, flips the cigarette past my face, through my open window. I'm digging for my seat belt. "Most people are too healthy," she says, running a yellow light. She lays on the horn. The wind through the windows keeps the litter in the backseat dancing.

In a blue-collar Washington suburb, in Maryland, Barrie parks the car, pulls her horn case from the backseat pile, and we start our date in the Brookwood High School gym. There has been a theme dance the night before. There are nets, human-sized crabs, car-sized dolphins, pots of real sea grass from the Maryland shore.

Barrie asks another French horn to make room for me then points out instruments of the Brookwood Community Orchestra—the bearded trumpet wires houses; the string bass markets

life: yogurt with active cultures, bee pollen, bran, new Bibles.
point to the slick-looking oboe. "Female surgery," Barrie frowns
"See his nails?" Barrie notes that the orchestra is rich with
clarinets and flutes—wives, mothers, unmarried teachers, and
single, black male, teenaged, grinning, flashing braces.

Barrie lifts her instrument, but before she sounds a warm-up
the oboe's beeper beeps and the doctor packs to leave. The con
ductor gravely nods, acknowledging for the orchestra a moment
of Science and Art. Music and Rumor.

Earl John Delhomme directs the Brookwood Community Or
chestra. His hair is short as a recruit's. His black oxfords shine
His feet are the size of a child's. Earl's belt and belt buckle an
shirt collar look large.

"His clothes seem dangerous for him."

"Earl John is," Barrie informs, "*ill*." Barrie next makes a poin
that it's stupid people who develop long illnesses. "You need mor
than indolence and selfishness," she says. "You need a stupi
endurance—*a beast's endurance*—to make a good patient, to b
expert at being sick."

"An ability to endure as the cause of unwanted illness? What
notion. That's some notion."

"I stole the notion from a poet, a good English poet. *Auden*.
thought I'd see if it'd fly. I think it's Auden," Barrie says. "He
the one who ended up with Lillian Hellman's face, right?"

Now, both arms waving from unbuttoned sleeves, Delhomm
dismounts his stand (an overturned trunk) to approach th
first ring of his orchestra—a little two-step, bird-bony hands i
flight. "Boy, I have a band," he confides. Eyes clamped, he hitche
his pants with his elbows. His hands climb and dip then climb
sliding in and out from his sleeves. Earl's skin is loose at th
wrists. Of a sudden, Earl John seems vandalized, calls a break.

Ed Bolling replaces his conductor atop the trunk, then begin
to make announcements. Ed Bolling's name is stenciled to th
music stands, typed on large white labels taped to individua
sheets of music and to their cardboard folders. Bolling distribute
mimeographed information that pronounces first in purple ink
From E. Bolling, Manager.

Barrie elbows me. "Ed Bolling is the manager of the Brook
wood Community Orchestra."

Earl John returns and the orchestra struggles through an hour. When sections of the orchestra have rests those musicians talk while the others play. During one break, Barrie oils the valves of her horn, which, she explains, is a product of the Germans.

"Then why would they call it French? You made that up."

"They were constructed first in Germany, not France," says Barrie.

"I suppose it doesn't matter, really."

"If you were German?"

Earl John Delhomme watches Barrie pack. He waves at us. I wave back. Earl rushes over, takes my hand, then raises and kisses Barrie's. The poor man seems naked. Barrie and I leave Earl John deserted in his practice room, standing near his stand—ballet bars on either flank, suburb women arriving in tiger tights—Bolling reporting in, collecting his conductor's music.

Barrie threads her arm through mine. In the car, I study Bolling's mimeoed sheet: *Information and Directions.*

"Mr. Delhomme is dying. Liver, lymphs. He told us, when he found out, that he wasn't sorry for anything in his life. Can you imagine? Anyway, I don't miss practice. I don't think he's a beast, but he has endurance."

Barrie whips a turn at an intersection, west. We both reach to fold down our visors. The sun seems to have stopped its setting to stall in our eyes.

The bottom third of E. Bolling's sheet is to be torn off and passed to the city police for parking in their lot the evening of the outdoor concert. Just above Ed's double dotted line: *If YOU reach Capitol Christian Church (on left), YOU have gone too far!*

When Barrie suggests we stop for beers, I give her a chary look.

"I'm not going to talk about my sisters."

We find a bar and table. First, we talk about the air-conditioning. I mention that in a book of essays, Gore Vidal dates the End of the Old Republic and The Birth of the Empire to the invention, in the late thirties, of air-conditioning. "Before air-conditioning, Washington was deserted all summer and early fall. But now, Congress can sit and sit and never stop making mischief." Then, because Barrie asks me, I explain again about the conference I've come to attend, about the computers, about teaching English.

"That's good, teach kids while they think they're watching TV."

"I suppose."

"But you're here. You don't believe in it?"

"I believe in some of it. I wanted to see some city art, eat city food, hear city music."

"If you really want to kill yourself," Barrie says, "you can."

"You said," I say, then head to the bar. I take my time ordering beer, get the whole rundown on selections. I start not to return to the table, but do. I hold up the beer, give Barrie her choice between Belgium and Holland.

Barrie scans me. "I'm off the pills," she says, then starts a story with her eyes closed: "Marie-Antoinette Cappucci was fifteen when she went to visit her brother in the Air Force in South Dakota. She came back *full*."

Barrie opens her eyes, crosses them, puffs her cheeks. She tells me she wants me to not be upset. She runs a list of words for me: *peeved, pestered, baited, nagged, gnawed, kindled, dandered.* "*Dander's* a word," she says, "is *dandered*?" She reaches for Holland. "The summer she came home, I was eight.

"In Marie's kitchen we watched Elvis on TV, Marie going crazy like this. Mrs. Cappucci's at the sink doing whatever she's doing there. Marie's going nuts. I'm going nuts. Marie loves Elvis. I love Elvis. *We* love Elvis.

"Mrs. Cappucci fished Marie shoes from the bottom of the bin at Filene's. I'd sit on Marie's bed and look in her closet at these zillions of shoes. Zillions. Marie had hoops in her skirts.

"Mrs. Cappucci cried and cried after Marie came back from her brother's, sat in my mother's kitchen. Guess what her brother's name is." Then: "Nino. What did you think it was?"

"Nino."

"What do you think he does? Take a big guess."

"Construction. Electrical work. Cement."

"He's a photographer," says Barrie. "He takes photos."

"*Photos* by *Nino*."

"She broke Sammy Taro's heart who loved loved loved her—

still loves her for all I know." Barrie stops to agree with herself. "Probably he still loves her."

Then: "There was Marie in her dress and everyone standing in her cruddy backyard. The Cappuccis had these two terrible trees and they had a hammock. The trees were too close to really hang the hammock, but they were the only two trees they had." Barrie shrugs.

"Marie came over to be by me in the hammock. We tried to sit, but then we got all balanced on our bellies to watch the feet lapping.

"'Jesusmaryandjoseph,' her mother cried. She hauled Marie to her feet, then handed her wine: 'Drink this!' Marie said, 'What?' then trailed her mother the rest of the night. I watched everything from the hammock. Marie got married. Mrs. Cappucci got drunk."

Barrie starts to take a rest, then says, "Marie-Antoinette Cappucci has six children by this Swede who has no reason for it except he has been in the Air Force with her brother. Pale, blond, dumb kids. Blue eyed." Barrie blows out air like she's been pressing weights, then gives me big eyes. "It takes Marie eighteen years to get over visiting her brother in South Dakota. South Dakota? Boy, do I know about South Dakota."

John W. Hinckley, Jr., is quoted in the *Washington Post*. He's shocked the jury found him not guilty by reason of insanity in the shooting of President Ronald Reagan and three others. Hinckley suggests he has been severely mistreated by being locked away. He admits, he says, he was insane when he fired on the four men, but feels, now, sane and "really sorry" for presidential aide James Brady, whom he head-shot.

But Barrie is more interested in Argentina. She's brought to my hotel a clipped article from the same paper I've been reading. She lifts my *Post* from the bed, points to the copy of her scissored piece. She reads from hers. "From London:"

Prime Minister Margaret Thatcher celebrates "the fine victory of our boys—a clear sign to the world." On the other hand,

London officials say, they were "surprised" by the Argentine surrender. "We were preparing ourselves for a pretty unpleasant battle at Port Stanley," quotes a Thatcher aide. The surrender was sudden but welcome, he allows.

British Losses:
23 aircraft
2 destroyers
2 frigates
1 supply ship
2 landing ships
243 dead or missing
333 wounded

"Unpleasant battle?" queries Barrie. She dashes to the TV. "Let's see it on the news. It's now." But it's not, and we have to wait for an hour. Barrie leaves the sound turned down. "I'm waiting for the English countryside."

We both wait. There's no choice.

"There it is!" Barrie cries. She leaps from the bed, twists the volume.

"Hip, hip, hooray!" a stout Englishwoman shouts, standing in her home by her telly. "The Empire'll not be toyed with!"

Unemployed textile workers are proud. "Hip, hip, hooray!" they shout from a pub, eyeballing the cameras.

Barrie and I have not made love. On the plane, in the terminal, the next two days, it seemed we might, but we've not. Waiting for the news from England, nothing has been kissed. The Falklands, a thousand and more miles south—its sheep and mud— seem more real than my room with this woman in it.

"The Empire Strikes Back!" Barrie agrees, pointing from the pillows, happy as the Brits. "I feel vexed," she sighs. "*Tea.*"

We find a four-star something or other in Georgetown, where after dinner, we move into its jazz bar. I order bourbon. Barrie drinks tea the bartender has to beg from the restaurant. "Do you think we'll make love?" she asks, poising her cup near her lips. She waits for my answer, then says, "We'll see."

"Hip, hip, hooray!"

"Why'd you do that?" Barrie says, then leaves.

I'm not unhappy to stay for the jazz.

The young black vibraharpist plays elliptical, delicate blues. He both backs and fronts the bassist's line—builds, strikes, retreats, returns. He glimmers. He knows, already, which notes *not* to play—an older man's game. At the end of the set, I collar him, offer drinks.

"Buy for the bass."

The bass is in his sixties and he accepts a drink, then stays after the second set. He gestures through the window. "Fog's moving in." Then: "From the Potomac."

I give the outside a good look myself, raise a toast. "To the Chesapeake Bay."

"The Atlantic."

"The fjords of Norway."

We mush our way on north, then south, both icecaps, pausing to name capes and straits and to add in Greenland.

The bass informs that Greenland is the largest island in the world and belongs to Denmark. "Eric the Red. Tenth century." The bass has lived in France and Holland, Finland, Denmark.

"To Eric."

"Eric."

I point out that the ice of the icecaps would be pure. "The Japanese tow glacier calves home to package and sell."

The bass asks how old is the ice? "This clean stuff?"

"One point eight million to ten thousand years ago—somewhere in there." The bass and I give it all what we think is ample pause and time, then hoist our drinks: "*To the Age of Glaciers.*"

"To them and their calves."

"To *that*—all that."

Eventually we buy the bottle, stand it on the table. The bass motions to, then calls the bartender. "Bottles get new glasses, man."

Which sounds like somebody's God's truth to me.

―――――――

After midnight, on TV, a Washington psychiatrist, a minister, and a Georgetown University sociologist earnestly discuss John Hinckley. The moderator is a Georgetown University law professor.

The minister glares and preaches. He has the advantage—at the moment—of being black, in the employ of God, of possessing a smooth and ruckless face. He seems, too, to have hired a reliable tailor.

The moderator requests a definition of *insane*. The psychiatrist informs, then lights a cigarette. The minister twists about. "The crazy shot four people." *Crazy* is the minister's word. He has placed it on the stage as object, a bird in hand.

There are few objects on stage other than this word and the chairs, the moderator's desk, a mutant green plant, the four hired minds. The lawyer-moderator fingers his mike.

The minister perseveres. "Hinckley had a pool. He could swim in his yard."

The psychiatrist flicks ashes, returns the minister's stare, draws on the cigarette. There are no ashtrays. The lawyer seems uncomfortable for, or about, the smoker. The lawyer remembers he is on TV, stops his looking about.

The sociologist smoothes her skirt, and the camera cuts to her. "If Hinckley's crazy (*there*, she has said *it* too), then so are all the rest of us. We're all trying to be seen."

The minister cries out: "Actions has consequences. Nobody jams in this world alone. Goddamnit."

The moderator is in live pain.

Some hours before, I'd announced to the bassist at the bar: "There's a country between love and self. Beats being alone."

"I watched the broad high-knee her way out—tell *her*," said the bass, then signaled for a cab, then installed me in back.

On the TV, the psychiatrist lights another cigarette.

I'm watching, but only half-listening. Eventually, the black minister calms down. I attended sessions of my conference all day, and I've not called Barrie. In the morning, I fly home. *To Whom It May Concern*, I pray aloud, drunk enough. I climb into bed. *I'll be a sun-bean for Him. Amen.*

When I get home, I write to Barrie. From Colorado, among other things, I bring up the Star Trek bar, the business about the suicide and the physics. She writes right back, and we start a postcard exchange. She ignores physics and Latin vocabulary. She even snubs South Dakota. She talks about God:

Both you and the Pope forget Christianity's Guy committed suicide. He set the example.

To love your neighbor as yourself makes no sense if to kill yourself is also permitted.

To live is to be tempted, which makes martyrdom attractive. My guess is a lot of the Christians the Romans fed to lions were volunteers.

So deal with it in the civil law then. If you're a judge, how do you handle a crime in which the aggressor and the object of aggression are one?

I am not a judge. My name is Barrie.

Maybe judges worry suicide is transposed murder. If someone is willing to kill himself, can he be trusted to spare another? See, we're back to loving neighbors.

What I'm saying isn't stupid.

What you're saying is life only works at The Grand Moment of Death. Are you reading too many French novels? Suicide's *not* vaudeville, for God's sake. When someone kills himself, he's gone. There's a word. Roll that out your mouth: *Gone.* Listen—no, really—have you tried analysis?

My analyst fell in love with me. He was more like a recreation director than a physician. Freud pegged it: the purpose of psychoanalysis is to convert hysterical misery into ordinary unhappiness.

What ever happened to Marie and the Swede and the kids?

The Swede retired from the Service, then left her.
After twenty years as a sergeant in the Air Force, he got
some big-deal deal in Iran. Boeing and the Shah hired him.
Mrs. Cappucci says no judge can touch him in his civilian
clothes in the Arabian desert. Marie goes out with a customer
at the bar she works at who has Elvis Presley sideburns. I
don't have to tell you what that looks like. It took Marie
eighteen years to get over South Dakota. I didn't tell you?

What I next send isn't a postcard. I write a fake diary, post that.
Barrie calls long distance: "Who said you could say this? Who
said?"

"I felt jealous of your analyst."

Barrie writes she's been reading a novelist new to her: John
L'Heureux.

He's good and is, as I understand it, a recovering alcoholic
and a self-defrocked priest.

I write back that I've read L'Heureux, but her note confirmed
why, of a sudden, I knew I preferred Graham Greene:

I vote Greene — an unrecovered alcoholic who wanted to be
a priest.

Then:

My father's best friend had a Black Lab dog, a champion
birder. When she got too old to hunt she killed herself by
drowning herself in the farm's pond. It's true. Belle — her
name was Belle — first tried to starve herself, but my father's
friend force-fed her. So Belle drowned herself. My father and
his friend were proud. Well?

I least admire art that disappears. I once watched some joke
in a beret install a block of ice the size of a kid's wagon on the

steps of a museum. Then he dumped dead leaves on the ice. Besides suffering from its own limitation, the melting ice and the leaves were dangerous. I'm surprised nobody cracked their skull.

Marie has married Elvis. Even with his paunch, my mother says, he's truly the one she should have married in the first place. Marie made a mistake, then spent almost twenty years to recoup. You don't think that's long?

There's nothing to life but life.

You can't escape the experience of your own experience.

What do you want me to say? that suicide's an act of ambition? It is—except of course for the fact that the act rockets you past ambition. It's an act that eats itself. What you live is your life.

Life?—here's life—straight from the papers:
Woman to marry man accused of trying to kill her:
A woman plans to marry the man accused of repeatedly stabbing her and breaking her arms with a hammer in an attempted murder.
Conner Wyatt, 20, and Justin Bradley Spears, 20, applied for a marriage certificate this month in Rochester, New York. Spears is charged with second-degree murder in the assault.
Wyatt was repeatedly stabbed with a screwdriver October 19 in the home the two shared. Her hands and arms were broken with a hammer.
Spears, who pleaded innocent, is being held in jail.
His father, Monroe County Sheriff's Deputy Brian Spears, said both families support the wedding.
"We're all in this as a family," he said Friday.

When I dream, I am a boy with my father in my uncle's car, an old Chrysler with FluidDrive. It is unclear where we are headed

Barrie (cont.) 131

in my uncle's blue car, but in the dream we are crossing Kansas. My father shakes me awake to see, in the distance, an overpass. My father, wobbled by the construction, wants me to see it. The overpass grows until we pass beneath it. My father threatens to stop my uncle's car. What he does is accelerate. There is a scent of something. I know because it's hot and the windows are rolled down. "Get your head in here," my father shouts, still mashing the gas. Then he softens, sends me to the backseat to look through that window.

The overpass has been perfectly constructed except that there are no roads to it—the bridge connects air. Each time I turn, my father's still glaring at this shoreless bridge in his mirror. He doesn't complain I'm blocking his view.

In time, the bridge drops below the horizon. My father backs off on the gas. He calls me to the front seat to explain the bridge disappears because the earth is not flat, but round. "Even Kansas," he says. He seems surprised himself.

My guess is the bridge is real—that I saw it with my father. That if I were to drive along long enough in Kansas, I'd sight it. Somewhere near Junction City, say, or Salina, or Wilson Lake, or Hays. The bridge would arrive. Or I would.

The perfect pointless construction astraddle a road, triumphantly idle: a sundial centered for a nation, an altar, a permanent needle of a compass facing north, an Andy Warhol joke, a perch for bird or locust, an unfinished road from home.

Barrie sends a postcard: *If you publish a book will you use an epigraph?*

I post a postcard back:

If you can't imagine yourself an SS officer hustling the Jewish women and children to the gas chamber, you need to be more closely in touch with your buried self.
—Paul Fussell

Barrie antes:

Fear of losing a woman and loving her are not the same thing.
—Russell Banks

Then:

. . . this is a book of memory, and memory has its own story to tell. But I have done my best to make it tell a truthful story.
—Tobias Wolff

You called for night; it falls: now cry in darkness.
—Samuel Beckett

Like most men, I tell a hundred lies a day.
—Vance Bourjaily

Faith, like a jackal, feeds among the tombs, and even from these dead doubts she gathers her most vital hope.
—Herman Melville

Kill the body, the head dies.
—Joe Louis

Morty . . . my marriage was a mistake. Most people's marriage is a mistake. Marriage is where people go to make your mistakes.
—Frederick Busch

Then:

Zip up your coat.

You could lose an eye.

You want something to cry about?

I'll give you something to cry about.

If I have to stop this car.

Barrie (cont.) <u>133</u>

mav·er·ick

---

mav·er·ick n. An unbranded or orphaned range calf or colt, traditionally considered the property of the first person who brands it. "Mav·er·ick" is a reader service of *The Montana Standard* and will be published whenever volume warrants.

I want to trade a Ping-Pong table, two registered female miniature dachshunds, and a pony for firewood. Leave message for Lyman. 633-5286.

I am looking for a tall aluminum Christmas tree and someone who can do Hawaiian or Polynesian dancing. I can trade stock tank/windmill repair. Call 633-0005.

I have a dead flowering plum tree to give to anyone who can remove it. Call Sherri, 473-5402.

I have a female hybrid wolf, good with children, to give away. Call 633-7063.

I am looking for the following items: World War II German army rifles (98K Mausers), preferably sniper rifles; a Reising Model 60 rifle; a good hunting rifle in 250 to 300 caliber; and ivory elk teeth. I can trade welding or small tree removal. I prefer to trade welding. Jake, 473-0948, weekends.

I want to trade 4,500 pieces of unused costume jewelry for a 1986 or newer economy car with air conditioning. I also am looking for good used oak furniture and a Lady Kenmore portable washer. I can pay, or trade jewelry. Winona, 633-5395.

I want to trade a four-year-old female Indian ringneck parakeet for other birds, preferably love birds. I can deliver. Sherri, 473-5402.

I have the following items to trade: a fertilizer spreader, clay flower pots, a boy's Sears bedspread with matching drapes and valance, a lady's vanity, and a one-man raft with oars. I am looking for any kind of gold-prospecting equipment and a saxophone in excellent condition. Call 633-8540.

I can trade iris rhizomes and peony bushes. I also have a 5-inch-diameter ball of string to give away. Call 633-2850.

I want to trade an eight-week-old guinea pig, three German black laying hens, a two-year-old neutered outside terrier-mix dog, and one lop-eared rabbit to homes with good cages for houseplants. Call 473-2759.

I am looking for a videotape of Oprah's show with Susan Lucci and "all her men" that aired last season. I can trade a tanning lamp with a five-minute timer. Sherri, 473-5402, after 4.

I want to trade two side-by-side spaces at Evergreen Park's "Garden of Angels" Mausoleum for a full-size American car or pickup. Call Al, 633-2384.

I am looking for the book "Living Proof: The Hank Williams, Jr. Story." I can pay a reasonable price. Call 633-6402.

I want to trade a 1967 Dodge automatic two-door for something. Call 473-2437, evenings.

I am looking for anyone who witnessed an accident at 7:30 p.m. Dec. 24 at the intersection of Granite and Silver. I am also looking for copies of any "Gunsmoke" episodes starring Burt Reynolds as Quint. Call 633-9840.

A church group is looking for a sausage press. Tax receipts available. Call 633-2855.

I want to trade a boy's guitar with a Lone Ranger decal for Mr. Peanut banks. Call 633-7526.

I am looking for a welded steel cab-over lumber rack for a full-size Jimmy. I can trade an AT&T answering machine and pay the difference. Call 633-9823.

Found a woman's diamond ring and a colored key chain with keys on a hiking trail near Big Timber. Key chain says "I Wuf You." Call to identify ring and keys. 473-9820.

I am looking for a home weight set with a bench and a pec deck. I can trade a child's 12½-inch bicycle with training wheels, acupuncture, window washing, or computer typesetting. Call 633-3974.

I am looking for a gentleman (in his 60s) to play pinochle with another man and two women. Call 473-3221, ask for Bliss.

I have three ducks to give away. Call 633-2850.

I am looking for a dog sled, harnesses and other gear. I can trade irrigating boots, dropshank spurs, snaffle bits, one good tooled saddle, or an air-conditioning setup for a Volkswagen Dasher. Call 633-8477.

I want a gas mask (man's), an Army helmet (man's), and a man's Army weapon, preferably a machete, and Army or Marine survival manuals. I prefer to trade welding, but can also pay. Jake, 473-0948, weekends.

I have a wedding dress (size 8, used once) in excellent condition to trade. Leave message on machine for Sherri. 473-5402.

If you have something to trade or give away or are looking for something out-of-the-way, write "Mav·er·ick," c/o *The Montana Standard*, Roundup, MT 59072. Requests must be brief and each request must be mailed separately. *Phone calls will not be accepted.*

Baby Teeth

On public TV I catch a documentary about a doc
umentary about war. The Israeli army has produced a film to
motivate and teach, even induce debate among its troops regard
ing what's to be encountered in war. Clear things: Death, Life
Victory, Defeat. And things less distinct: the greasy morality o
battle, the issuing of orders, the murky and extended busines
of survival and innocence and control. How not to admire th
audacity of such a training film for soldiers? Though how woul
anyone other than the Israelis dare to do it? Like anyone wh
has seen it—been near it, *in* it—I know that ignorance has it
place in battle, know it probably belongs. Still, I hear mysel
say. *Still.*

I expect to see on TV dust and fire. Confusion. Closeups. Steel tank tracks, say, crushing stone. There ought to be battle images, but what appears is the ever so sharply focused face of a handsome Frenchman. He is the director of the film about the Israelis' film. His unmarked face fills the screen. He discusses war as *Idea* in a way that suggests that war is, first and foremost, a question of Technological Aesthetics. Leave it to the French.

The Frenchman knows he is great looking. He knows the face on the screen. The pull to be in the movies: to join the audience? to see your own face as large as a door? To be fair, I will say the man seems persuaded by more than his looks—in fact, speaks as if he has, against reason, gotten his hands on some secrets he wants me to know. But how not to suspect him? Like a priest explaining women, the director explains war, using what he has at hand: *words*. Shock, Dread, Nausea, Heart, Majesty, Perversion, Honor, *Self*-expression. The French accent manages, I notice, to assign the abstractions Force. The mere words sound charmed, self-contained and alive, and unnerving, like poems.

Eventually, the Frenchman dissolves and I watch the Israeli soldiers and the Lebanese civilians who portray themselves on screen. I sense the blood moving in the soldiers' bellies. And each time a soldier jams a clip into his weapon, I hear it. The sound is like the sound of a baseball rocketing off a bat. The sound is distorted. It is Hollywood: *Krack!*

In my chair in my living room I'm huffing as though I've been humping for miles, full pack. As though one of the soldiers, I shoot a look at the TV sky, scan for fire. Some aged rumor seems verified, but which one? Is what I feel Loss? I close my eyes to the set's glare and begin to regulate my breathing. I explain things to myself. There are men older than I who have survived Knowledge. What is this TV program to me, this concoction? Years have passed since doctors tenderly examined for shrapnel as though they were hunting budding teeth. Years since they waited for the teeth to erupt like a baby's treasure. Poor inflamed gums. Festered gums. *Poor baby*. It was a Filipino doctor who called my eruptions teeth, babies' teeth. He thought he was a poet.

The wounds which blanket me, like the Shroud of Turin, form cloudily an imprint. Not the imprint of one man but the imprint of entire cities. Map grids. Hue. Quang Tri. Khe Sanh. Cities. *My* metaphor. Let the doctor have his. In recurring dream, intent on shaping my end of things, I search the old cities for one holy man but without luck. The cities seem searchable by grid, but I don't find him. Even from the height of dream, I never find him. I see the old cities on my skin: places of fire and plague, of corruption, overcrowding, brooding—*cities as sores*, not entirely a medieval notion—and feel the ancient desire to set sail for green land. But there is no ship. There is no holy man and there is no ship.

I have seen, too, on my neck, chest, and naked belly an image like an old engraving of Lyndon Johnson on the floor of the Oval Office, on the rug, with his own sheaves of maps planning, with his generals, attacks. One of the generals is a sweet-faced Air Force one-star. He looks about to remove his shiny black shoes. He is reaching for the laces. The President, sitting on the floor, watching, crosses his stocking feet.

Henry Shrapnel survived his creation to a ripe and fine age: eighty-one. Unhonored during his military career for his invention, he was promoted near life's end to the rank of lieutenant general. Years hence, his weapon proved in particular effective in the full trenches of World War I. Time has refined the original hollow shell packed with musket balls and powder, but the idea was first Henry's. He survives. You might know him. I know him. Generations of close-packed bodies of men on their hunkers know him. Like any artist, he exists in his work.

I consider getting up to construct a drink, but don't: I feel assigned to the set—on *duty*—my shift. I watch the TV for signal puffs of smoke and the high-angled descent of mortars. I have lost even in my home, in the comfort of my home, any balm of Distance. The camera won't permit it. Besides planned and expected vistas—pans of cluttered landscape and what seems general and continuous fire—the camera turns and turns to the *single* human face, faces cropped from among the soldiers and the civilians, fetched up for the screen. The faces press against the screen like night wind against windows. The faces work their ways into my home and my room.

I wish to remove my clothes. To seem more one of the soldiers? To confirm, though marked, I've been spared? I remove the clothes. Empty wells abound. Dry city wells. Or poisoned ones

Or potholes. What's the difference? *I have lost my teeth.* See. This is my life. See.

As a child I believed in, even resented, the indestructibility of objects. What day was it when I finally knew better? How old was I? Even so, now older, now wiser, I wish for each face on the screen some accompanying object I can trust—something that will not in an instant wither or fade or break. *Something to survive its owner.* I want to see things together. A face and a jewel? A face and shoes, sturdy shoes? A face and a metal dog tag? But all I'm offered are the solo and naked faces, the heads: nerves, and nerve roads, and blood: soup housed by bone the size and the strength of a bowl.

The Faces, even the women's—especially the women's—seem, in time, unsafe to gaze on, like Lot's wife. The filmed land, too, reflects this logic of salt and fire. What trees there are are green, but appear, despite the mummery, parched, exhausted. In the air, in my home, is the dirty, scorched smell of my mother's laundry room. Or was it her mother's? I inhale, not knowing whether the burned odor is memory or fact.

Soon a Lebanese woman's neighborhood is "stormed," but the woman—*the camera on her face*—is unmoved by the event. The woman's face is as unscored and as beautiful as old stone. Like such stone, she is more caked with age than she shows. And this: She has the proud, invaded look of a sharecropper's face: a photo by Walker Evans. The mackerel eyes. But how is it—how has her face escaped, in this desert all the years, wind and sun? Unalert to her own beauty (could it be true?), she eyes the crack troops as they storm (first through dry fields) the cluster of homes where she lives (something in the construction of the houses glitters, shines like light). The Israeli director lifts a wrist to order a burst of firing to startle the cast. The trained troops, suddenly script-less, dive for cover, but the woman, erect in a backless kitchen chair outside her door, does not. She stares beyond the downed soldiers. I stare where she stares: the far color is white-yellow, as though the horizon sky has been glassed with plastic badly damaged by heat. In fact, I see now that the full dome of the sky looks coated. Were it night, you would not see planets or stars. You would feel alone.

The Israeli director's disappointment with the pretty woman who stares swells like the gathering of shot nerves or weather. "God, Goddamnit, God damn it," he issues through clamped teeth: a punished schoolboy forced to conjugate verbs. What had he expected from this, his unbargained-for beauty, his discovered star—sudden haughty coal eyes? a blooded bottom lip? a Hollywood cry for mercy? The director, a member of the Israeli Defense Forces film division, turns to the handsome foreign director of the shadow documentary of his own. "Too long in real life," he diagnoses for the Frenchman, "No go. Not a go." The Israeli has bared his teeth and they shine like bone. "Fuck it," he says and wets his lips, employing the curled stiff tip of his tongue. I expect the Frenchman to croak out something about truth being more scheming than lies, but he doesn't. He shoves his hands into baggy pockets, squints. He looks rested, face tight from soap. He has shaved. He looks great in the pressed army drab. The Israeli, in his drab, and with the teeth and the rough beard, looks cruel. And: the hawkblack eyes. The lifted upper lip. The hard hook of the nose. The tongue looks as strong as a spoon. The conserved motion of the Israeli's face—his teeth shutting down on words— puts you in mind of an efficient commando working two days on no sleep. His uniform is unpressed. The Israeli looks tired and uncoddled—a small, effective man without hope or second thoughts: a special danger I've witnessed before. I clench— a child who knows he'll be dropped—stop my breathing. But there's no wall of hard sound, no concussion. Still I wait. I can hear my heart pump.

On TV the Israeli folds his arms, crosses them, as though the world were impaired or, worse, were a stupid student. He aims his face toward the sky, then closes his eyes as if he has just shut windows. With deliberate pauses, he breathes. He sways a bit, blind. He begins to extend his arms for balance, then opens his eyes, wide and afraid, as after prayer, or the high spray of flak or rockets.

Here and there, flattened soldiers lift their heads, then, detecting the directors standing, exposed, pop up. The Israeli lowers his gaze from the heavens to the village. Then, once again looking resentful and insulted, focuses, like his beautiful civilian from her door, well beyond the soldiers. He is searching. For what? I can see all around the heat rise. Desert air like jungle air, it comes to me, has Authority and Jurisdiction. The air thinks it is God. Without notice, all grows quiet. Heaven and Earth. Has the soundtrack been doctored? Or no? Now, bare, thin arm aloft: "Cut." The Israeli thrusts the arm up, as if piercing the sun's wash toward other gods—Jehovah, Allah, Zeus, Mars—though whether in warning, or in fear, or in tribute, is uncertain. There is, though, clearly this: an awesome, chroming silence; and canalless sand; and rubble; and a single arm upraised, coppered, frail as a reed. Ah, I say to myself, and to anyone who might listen or hear, Yes. Ah.

Luck

My large intestine burst. I made it to the hospital, where the emergency room diagnosis was kidney stones. Bu
when a nurse administered a morphine injection which caused n
effect, it raised some eyebrows. A second injection failing to provide relief, coupled with a plunging blood pressure and a rocketing white blood count, caused a panic that, despite the haze o
exquisite pain, was not lost on me. Someone rushed off for a sur
geon, who showed up straight from surgery. His mask was un
tied, but his cap was in place, and there was blood on his greens
"We're going in," he announced. At the time, believe this or not
all I could think of was Walter Mitty—"*We can't make it, sir. It
spoiling for a hurricane, if you ask me.*" "*I'm not asking yo*

Lieutenant Berg," said the Commander. "Throw on the power lights! Rev her up to 8,500! We're going through!"

When I woke, there was Dr. Mitty. He pressed a palm to my forehead, then pulled a tube from my nose. I felt the tube jerk up my throat. The surgeon next drew the sheets back. I was shown the flesh of my colon, now stitched with black thread to an aperture in my belly. The organ, if that's what it was, appeared to be breathing. The surgeon had removed an arm's length of shredded intestine.

"Looked like chopped liver—shit everywhere!" The surgeon caught himself, then pointed out I'd been being poisoned to death and bleeding, which explained the blood pressure and white count. "Had to flop it all out, shower you down. Tromped around in there pretty good."

Beside the pink-fleshed opening was a stapled incision the length of a ruler. I covered myself, pulled up the sheet. Later, a child-nurse—Mindy Tarlett—came to visit, "to help me cope with my *trauma*." She began like a children's book: "What is an *Ostomy*?" Then: "An ostomy is a general term for an operation in which an artificial opening is created for the elimination of bodily waste. Ostomies are performed due to disease, congenital anomalies including cancer, inflammatory bowel disease, injury."

"Cancer?"

"Your physician will inform you."

"My physician told me this: 'There was shit everywhere!' Your people teach you to come in here and drop words like *cancer*, then bop on with the show? Why don't you go find my physician? Ask him if he forgot to tell me I have cancer? OK, Mindy?"

Mindy came back with an ICU nurse. This nurse babied a chart in her arms. She wanted to explain, she said, *diverticulitis*—an inflammation of diverticula in the intestinal tract, causing fecal stagnation and pain. "In your case," she said, "the diverticula had become so advanced that, like ulcers, they ate their way through your colon, your intestinal wall. You don't have cancer."

"No, but I can see my ass now without using a mirror."

"Well, yes, there is that," said the nurse. She gave me a look and a fairly normal smile. "You'll get through it," she said. "Mindy's here to help." The nurse was back in a minute. "Dr. Coates," she said, "had already performed seven surgeries when you came to

ER. As a young surgeon, he worked for the Peace Corps in Nepal, where he cut from dawn till dusk, without paperwork or fear of malpractice. He's seen and done it all. You were lucky to get him. He saved your life." She moved to my bed, leaned across my abdominal drain tubes, IVs, catheter. "Be nice to Mindy," she mouthed.

Mindy told me a surgical opening called a *stoma* is made in the abdominal wall and the end portion of the colon—"or intestine," she said, "some people don't know the large intestine is the colon. Anyways, the end portion of the colon is brought outside to the skin surface."

Mindy turned to the catalogs she'd brought. In these books were the *appliances*—adhesive flanges and plastic bags you could snap on to shit in. She walked through the procedures of preparing the skin around the stoma for the adhesive flange. *Cleanse the peristomal area with water and pat dry thoroughly, making sure it is free from any greasy substance or solvent. When Stomahesive Paste is indicated, apply a ring of paste to the back of the skin barrier, around the pre-cut opening. Allow the paste to set for one minute prior to application to skin.* Mindy next discussed ostomy pouches—bags—began with the high end: Designer Pouches.

"*Designer?*"

"Yes, colored pouches—mauve, night blue, amber—tiger pouches, elephant pouches . . ."

"Elephant?"

"Yes, elephant," she said. "And leopard." Mindy pointed out there were plain pouches too.

"Tupperware. I'm shopping for Tupperware," I said.

"Well, they are airtight," Mindy said. Then: "In the plain pouch line, you have transparent and opaque, and you have disposable and reusable."

"Opaque and disposable. Buy those, Mindy, sink my money into those."

Mindy penned a kind of contented note and moved on to Diet Tips for the Person with a Colostomy: "Loose bowels may be caused by larger, more liquid meals eaten at extremes of temperature, as well as green beans, broccoli, spinach, spiced foods, raw fruits, and beer. Gas production may be caused by foods from the cabbage family, onions, beans, cucumbers, radishes, and beer. Odor-producing foods include cheese, eggs, fish, beans, onions, vegetables of the cabbage family, some vitamins or medications, and asparagus. Reduction in fecal odor may be obtained by consuming cranberry juice, buttermilk, or yogurt." Mindy asked if I had questions about the substance of her briefing or the medical terminology.

"No, Mindy Tarlett. No."

"Mr. Mann, I'm here to help you accept your colostomy."

"I've no intention of accepting it. I don't goddamn like it, and I don't accept it." Then: "Ms. Tarlett."

When Mindy launched into her discussion of the protocol of Sex for Ostomates, I threw her out.

The ICU nurse came to tell me Mindy was crying, then said, "Wouldn't we feel better if we shaved?" She had a basin of water and a razor and soap.

"No, we wouldn't," I said.

When Dr. Coates came by the next morning, I thanked him for saving my life and thanked him again when he said that in six to eight months, he figured he could reconnect the separated colon. "It was pretty traumatized," he said. "We're going to let it rest, then reconnect it. I'm going to tell you something," he said, "and you can take it to the bank. Everybody has more colon than they need. We could do this again—just kidding," he said. "See you tomorrow. We'll pull a couple of tubes." He touched the draining lines.

What I knew was this: whatever way I was to cut it, it was going to be impossible to jaunt about feeling cool and invulnerable with a plastic bag of shit hanging from my gut. Calling a bag of shit an appliance wouldn't change its spots.

───────

At two weeks old, I fell into convulsions, turned blue. My grandmother (my father's mother) filled two buckets—one with cold water, one with warm—and began to alternately immerse me. My mother (she was not yet twenty), called the doctor, a newly immigrated Swiss, who dispatched the city ambulance. At work underground at the mine, my father couldn't be reached. By

the time my father finished his shift, the doctor had admitted me
to the hospital and informed my mother that I would die, news
my mother passed to my father.

My father said, "No—won't let him." According to my mother,
my father expended the night in prayer, though this was not his
characterization. Over the Swiss doctor's protestations, my father
carted me home at dawn, still made it to work on time.

When I was sixteen weeks, my mother was changing my dia-
pers and I got away. I crawled off the bed, struck my head on
the floor. I began to convulse but came out of it, my mother dip-
ping me into cold and warm water. She told me these stories recently. "I could have died," she said, "when it happened again.
The convulsions."

"Did you tell Dad?"

"I don't remember. Maybe not."

On a pleasant fall day, I'd left work early. Though I wasn't
thinking of it at the time, my exit off the interstate had been the
scene of a shooting some weeks before. A driver had cut off another in traffic and a chase had ensued. At the exit, the pursuing
driver forced the other driver off the shoulder, then fired at the
car seven times. One of the hollow-point slugs killed the driver.
The shooter was an unemployed electronics worker. He was
black, the dead man white. And the shooter had not been alone—
his wife and daughter had been with him. All this was milked on
local TV.

As I came upon the site of the shooting, my glasses were covered by whatever had just happened, and I couldn't see. For an instant I thought I'd been blinded, then saw beneath the rims of my
glasses. I inspected my chest and lap—*all gore*—dropped my chin,
peered over the rims. The windshield, darkened, had folded in
like a quilt. I slowed, sensed the road's shoulder, stopped, pulled
the key, scrambled out. I removed my eyeglasses, wiped them
with my thumb.

Ahead, a semi had slammed to a stop, slid off the road and to
a rest, like me, on the sandy shoulder. The driver, gut waving,
seemed to be charging at me under water. He wore a travel-

stained ball cap: DEKALB Genetics, which he tipped when he stopped. He seemed peculiarly formal.

"I've been shot." I felt I should explain.

"No. Smacked a deer. You OK?"

I turned to my Bronco II. The windshield—the *safety* glass—had, as I say, sagged in, but all the rest of the glass was broken.

The trucker sat me on the running board of the passenger side. He had a towel. "Now let's see which is your blood, which hers," he said, pointing up the road. Fifty yards up the shoulder lay a doe.

"You're kidding," I said, stood up. The trucker escorted me to the doe, lifted the hind legs: "A hundred twenty—thirty—pounds?"

The deer was halved, connected only by spine bone. The body cavity was wet sculpture: all soft organs and blood in my Bronco or on me. Of a sudden, I could taste, gagged all the way back to the Bronco. The interior appeared as if a pipe bomb had dismembered people.

The trucker sat me back down. By now, EMT people had arrived. And a cop. The tempered glass, blown from the driver-side window, had cut my head and ear, but it looked worse than it was. Most of the blood was the doe's.

The cop was looking things over. Because I was again sitting on the running board, the passenger-side door open, he was peering past my head. "Fuckin' lucky," he opined, then turned to the trucker. The trucker had begun to explain things. "Out of the bluffs," he said, pointing across the road to the hills.

"They come through here," the cop nodded. He motioned from the bluffs, across the road, then toward I-25, the front range of the Colorado Rockies. "Guy creamed one on 25—*came right through*—tore his fuckin' head off. Fuckin' lucky," he said.

"Out of the bluffs," the trucker said. "Car coming the other way, an old Olds. Deer jumped—completely skied it—landed *here*." The trucker fingered the post on the driver's side that supported the Bronco's roof and separated the front windshield from the driver-side door and window. "Hit midribs. Hindquarters crushed the door, forequarters crushed the windshield. Saw it."

"Rest of the glass?" asked the cop.

"Deer was *in* the car," said the trucker.

"*In?*" I said.

"Once she hit the post here, she flung around, like a nunchuk or such. Entered here." He poked his hand through the smashed side vista window. "Wheeled in there."

The trucker took the time to point out the slashed headliner, the kicked-out back window, all the missing passenger-side glass. He walked to the passenger side: "Came out here." He was standing beside the passenger-side back vista window space. I was still sitting on the running board. "She entered your car," he said, "then left it." We both looked up the road at the doe. City workers were tossing her into the back of a pickup. The trucker clucked his tongue: "You were in the one safe place there was. Saw it all."

The cop had turned his back, scanning traffic over on the interstate. A light rain had begun to fall. He was wearing a yellow slicker, POLICE stenciled across his back. The EMTs had cleaned me up. They were surprised at my normal blood pressure but were still trying to talk me into a trip to the hospital. I asked the tow-truck driver for a ride home. He gave me a look. "Near here?"

One of the EMTs asked if someone was home. "There can be a delayed reaction. You be careful, OK?"

While the tow-truck driver was fooling with chains and safety lights, I took a turn about the Bronco myself. Except for the driver's door being crushed and jammed (I did not recall scrabbling over the gearshift and passenger seat to exit), the only damage was to all the glass and the interior.

"Fell out of the sky," I said, "never saw it." I turned to the cop. "Might as well have been a meteorite. A bullet. Never saw it."

The cop folded his slicker, settled into his car, buckled up, motored off. He had waved a goodbye. The deer was gone, the trucker was gone, the EMTs, the cop. It was just me and Mr. Tow Truck, which was painted on the silver rig's doors.

---

convulsions, pathological body condition characterized by abnormal, violent, and involuntary spasmodic contractions and relaxations of the voluntary muscles, taking the form of a fit. Convulsions may be a symptom resulting from various diseases; e.g.

uremia, eclampsia, rabies, tetanus, hysteria, epilepsy, strychnine poisoning, cerebral tumor, and other conditions. They are usually accompanied (but not always) by unconsciousness. Popularly, the term is commonly restricted to the infantile variety, occurring in association with causes that upset the child's nervous system. Treatment should be prompt and include quiet rest, prevention of injury from falling and from biting the tongue or cheek, bodily warmth and comfort. *Medical advice is essential.*

In the hospital I asked Coates, who referred me to an internist. "What do I do to keep this from happening again?" I was a vegetarian at the time and a committed runner. The internist suggested a high-fiber diet and exercise.

I should explain the reversal: The Reconnection. I'll tell you now I spent more time in the hospital for the second surgery than for the emergency first. At rest eight months, my bowels had forgotten their work. And then there was the morphine.

When I woke after the first surgery, one of the cheers had been the available drugs. I was IVed into a drug machine I controlled. Computerized, the machines wouldn't let you overdose. But: you were in charge—didn't have to wait or ask for a nurse. I've been since informed that research supports that patients in charge of their own narcotics use less. But what I knew then—*and know now*—requires no study: whatever pain has to teach is unworthy.

Each day after the second surgery, I felt worse. In time, I came to understand that my body's wastes were rising and that my reconnected bowels misunderstood. I began to projectile vomit. The force of it all seemed dangerous, and the pain from the heaves made me sweat. The nausea caused by the constantly building bile felt almost impossible to face. I was weeping when the head nurse came into my room with equipment. She had a six-foot tube coiled in ice in a rectangular tray. The tube was transparent. Nurse sat me upright in a straight-backed chair in the center of the room and began feeding the tube up my right nostril. She'd asked if I had a preference, left? right? I'd raised my right wrist.

The tube had been packed in the ice to stiffen—but not too stiff—because, as Nurse pointed out, it had to make the turn to descend by way of the throat to the stomach. Nauseous beyond any nausea in my life, the tube being force-wormed down my throat worsened all. Nurse kept saying, "Help me, Mr. Mann." She had me nipping at water from a minicup. In theory, this sacramental nipping was to help me not resist the tube. In time, the tube was installed by way of my left nostril (Nurse abandoning the attempt through the right), down my throat, to and through the cardia, into the well of my stomach. I wept throughout the procedure.

Returned to my bed, I was connected to some sort of jar and suction. I watched the silage from my stomach travel through the tube to its new container. As before, I was IVed into my own narcotics. But despite this availability, I was unable to sleep, what with the tube poled in my throat and the pain of the surgeon's most recent invasion. Flesh had torn at the staples during the powerful vomiting. Blood beaded along the length of the incision.

On a late-night station, I watched a documentary about a Vietnam vet who, finding himself unfit for the company of people, was making it his life's work to study *Ursus arctos horribilis*, the grizzly. The program, as I recall, was shot in Glacier National Park, where it straddles Alberta, Canada, and the United States as it exists in northwestern Montana, my birth state.

Coates came by on his morning round: "Sorry—this usually occurs."

"What?" It wasn't easy to talk.

"The stomach pump—whatnot."

"If it usually happens, why didn't you install the tube before I came out of surgery, while I was asleep? Christ, Coates—you know? Had a tube in me the first time. Am I right?"

"That was an emergency. There was food in your gut—we didn't want you vomiting under gas. As for now—well—all patients don't need to be pumped. It doesn't *always* happen."

"No, just *usually*," I said. Which I meant and didn't. I owed Coates. What's more, I liked him.

"You need to wean off the pain killer. Narcotics paralyze— that's how they work—and we need the bowels to wake up. The pump here'll keep the sewage down, but we need the bowels to wake up."

"And the pain?"

"Have to choose," Coates said. "Up to you. The sooner the bowels rouse, the sooner we jerk the pump. The sooner we can jerk it." He lifted the jar as if to study the sludge. "I know it's no fun."

"I may have opted for the shit bag had I known what fun." I ask for a shot for nausea. I wanted something out of the visit.

"Sure," Coates said, "but do what you can to limit the narcotics." He tapped my machine.

It took three days for my bowels to rouse. I worked at stretching the stretches of time between my self-administration of what I guessed was morphine. I knew it'd been morphine on the first go-around. On the second, no one said.

I kept thinking of the vet and his grizzlies. Throughout the documentary all you saw was the man or a bear. I wondered how large the film crew had been, and how long they'd stayed (there were season changes in the film), and what had led the loner vet to permit the intrusion?

At home, I threw away what was left of my appliances. It dawned later I should've donated the stuff to someone—surely there were poor people with colostomies, people forced to re-usable bags.

Over a period of weeks, the hole in my belly closed.

---

diverticulum, intestinal, abnormal pocket in the wall of the intestine, found singly or in large numbers along the small intestine but more frequently along the colon. Diverticulosis occurs in 5 to 10 percent of persons over forty years old; its cause is unknown. In about 20 percent of persons with diverticulosis, the diverticula become inflamed, and, in severe cases, there is bleeding and perforation of the intestinal wall. Surgical removal of infected portions of the colon may become necessary.

A year before my father died—four heart attacks in fourteen hours—he called to recount the end of Jim Burl. I knew Jim too. As a kid, I'd worked for him in the woods. He'd leased some timberland outside Butte, Montana. The summer I turned seventeen, I and a half-dozen other high school boys were living in the woods, working for Burl. We bunked on the floor of a one-room cabin. We worked on growing beards. We wore long-sleeved flannels and watch caps. We'd bought rawhide belts and new gloves.

On Sundays, my father drove out to pitch in. He would get there in time to cook breakfast. He'd helped Jim rig up a saw using an old Dodge engine. It was a stripped-down truck with a mill blade connected direct-drive to the transmission. One of us boys would start the engine, confirm the gears into third, but when Jim and my father sawed, they kept us at bay. "You could lose an eye," my father said. He pointed to his. "I should know." Dad wore safety glasses he'd brought from the mine. Big Jim wouldn't wear them.

I still see the big saw sawing. "Eye, hell," I said even back then, "you could lose your head." The saw could have parted a horse. On one side of the blade, at a distance, we boys stacked logs; on the other side, we stacked the rough lumber.

As I write this I'm older than my father at the time he was covered with sawdust and risking his head. When I think of it now, I wonder how my father and Jim kept themselves intact. It was not they were careless so much as they were in those woods, in general, in a rush. What were they racing—time? bills? weather? luck?

When my son was ten, he spent two summer weeks with my parents. My father, retired from the mines, was landscaping on the side. He took Daniel along on his lawn and tree jobs. Telling Daniel to stand back, my father reached under a running lawn mower to dislodge wet grass. Too much in a hurry to shut the motor off, he mowed two fingers.

According to Daniel, my father wrapped his hand in a shirt, then draped the hand out the truck window as he drove. At the intersection of Harrison and Yale, he stopped to drop Daniel for the four-block walk home. "Don't tell Grandma," he said. "I'm going to the hospital. She'll fuss. I rescued your father from there once." He told Daniel to watch for traffic.

Daniel walked the four blocks home, then hung about in the yard. When my mother saw him, she asked where my father was. Daniel told her. My mother told me what my father said when she found him in St. James Emergency. He gave her a look. *"Where you been?"*

Jim Burl, my father informed, drowned. Jim and his son, Gary, had been winter fishing. The ice gave way along the edge of the Whitefish River and Jim was swept away. From upstream, Gary, on ice that looked the same but was safe, watched the current catch, then his father battle as his waders filled, then disappear. Jim wasn't found until spring. He'd been a nervy and powerful man. Here's a picture:

There were the odd-sized leftovers from the pine Jim and my father had rough-cut into eight- and ten- and twelve-foot planks. I and the other boys, in teams of twos and threes, had been loading these stumps into the chest-high bed of a large truck. Jim sold these stumps as waste to the paper plant. In this picture I'm painting, Jim selected a stump his own girth. It must have weighed three hundred pounds. He huffed, then lifted the stump, then set it in the truck like a biscuit. His face and scalp reddened, and his neck veins plumped. That was the summer my father shot a black bear male when the bear attacked the camp dogs. Two of the dogs died too. A third, a sweet black Lab bitch, late to the fight, lost a foreleg. She healed. She could run just fine but would topple when she walked.

---

chuck-a-luck (chùk′e-lùk′), noun. A gambling game in which players bet on the possible combinations of three thrown dice. [Probably chuck + luck.]

After they spliced the colon, I still had the belly hole, unclosed. You think of skin as thin flexible covering, like imitation leather or something, when in fact it's a complex organ.

"Dermis—not be confused with *epidermis*," said Nurse. "*Dermis*, not normally thought of as skin," she said, "is. It's the under-layer and consists of connective tissue containing blood vessels, lymphs, nerve endings, glands, fat cells, hair follicles, muscles. See how thick?"

I thought of Mindy Tarlett, but at least Nurse seemed more interested in supplying information than in helping me cope—though it seemed important to Nurse that I take a good look at the hole. I looked. I could *see* my *skin*. It made me lightheaded.

Twice a day, Nurse stuffed the hole with thin strip gauze soaked in a sterile saline solution—something, she said, learned in Vietnam. She'd served there. "Less chance for infection."

I didn't get what she was saying. "What?"

"To not close large wounds, to leave them heal open. *Less chance for infection.*"

"Oh."

"In the Nam, they stopped stitching up holes and just stuffed them. Like they did with our heads. Look how they stuffed us. Ever since Adam, we've been naming things, but, God, would Adam have named an *invasion* a consented *intervention*? A *killed* soldier," Nurse said, "is not a *neutralized* one. They were especially inventive, don't you think? My sister was a Marine nurse—*I was Army*—and she wrote that the Corps changed *booby trap*, because it made Marines feel dumb, to *surprise firing devices*. I told you what killed my sister, right? *Friendly fire.*"

She hadn't told me. I shook my head.

"Well, I'm telling you, words have power. You think *friendly fire* isn't a powerful conception?"

---

ileus, impairment of the caudad flow of the intestinal contents. Symptoms are a function of the level of obstruction and the type of ileus. Paralytic ileus is first evident through abdominal distention and vomiting.

Mr. Tow Truck dropped me at home. I held my briefcase, and two shirts and a suit I'd meant to drive to the cleaners. Everything slimed. A neighbor or two saw the Bronco being towed and assumed I was dead. My next-door neighbor told me I stood on my curb after Mr. Tow Truck left. In time, I headed up my driveway towards the garage. I lifted the lid from the garbage and dumped the briefcase, suit, shirts. I next stripped, dumped all that in the can. My neighbor said my clothes had been bloodied, front and back. Naked in my own backyard, I ran the garden hose on my head, then on my hands and two shoes. I gargled hose water.

In dream, I crossed a continent of ice that cracked but didn't give way. When I woke in the morning, there were streaks on my sheets. Glass in my hair had cut me. Careful as I was, when I washed my hair in the shower, I nicked my fingers. I felt lucky.

Barrie (cont.)

———

The first time I travel to D.C. after Barrie
death, the city is annealed, so paralyzed by ice that I'm forced t
a hotel in a Virginia suburb near Dulles Airport. The timing o
the storm is such that the plane lands, and in the minutes it take
to retrieve my baggage, then hail a cab, a freezing rain ha
achieved a coating. From the cab, and through the rain, Dulle
International recedes, becomes a bowl of light. Barrie woul
have had some facts. *Finn*-ished posthumously, she would hav
punned, thumb jabbing at the terminal. Then: *Saarinen's use o
steel cable takes advantage of its high tensile strength to suppo
large expanses of roof and at the same time provide large areas o
column-free space.* She would have waved at all the glass and th

concrete ribs installed to frame the glass to relieve stress on the cables.

The farther we inch from Dulles the more I unbottle a vision—my little movie of Barrie's church, the priest, his yews and mulberries. After that trip to Washington, I'd looked up *yew—evergreen tree or shrub of the family Taxaceae, somewhat similar to hemlock but bearing berrylike fruits instead of true cones. Of somber appearance,* I now almost instruct my Nigerian cabbie, *with dark green leaves, yews have been associated with death and funeral rites since antiquity. The wood of the English yew was used for the longbows of English archers, and the wood of several species is still so used,* which I'd written to Barrie.

She'd written back:

The Pacific, or Western, yew (T. brevifolia), *native to the NW U.S. and British Columbia, is valued for its bark, which is processed to yield paclitaxel* (Taxol), *a drug appropriate to treat ovarian cancer.*

When the cabbie and I leave the toll road to Washington for a hotel in Herndon, Virginia, the driver himself takes a room. The rain passes, but leaves all plated. My hotel windows are armored. Like a kid, I venture out.

In a restaurant a few blocks from the hotel, I am the sole customer. The telephone rings and rings. With elaborate apology, the mother or daughter refuses to make home deliveries. The mother has sent her sons, the drivers, home. She explains all this when, at the counter, I order souvlaki, salad, beer. The woman has four sons, two daughters. All but one of her sons are married, and the daughter working in the restaurant is the last child to live at home.

The daughter, a thin twin of the mother, seats me away from the door. The mother, from beside the phone on the counter, calls my order towards another door. The husband comes out to see who I am, then leaves to prepare the food. The daughter fills a glass with beer, but the mother carries it to me, then the daughter serves the food.

The mother brings a separate plate of extra peppers because when I'd seen them in the salad, I'd said I liked them. When I tell her I've walked from my hotel and will walk back, she seems relieved. She shakes a finger, "Not a night for driving." When I ask how she and her husband and daughter will get home, she points up, "A short walk. A safe one." She means for me to enjoy my dinner.

A customer enters. When the door chimes, the mother and I look at him, then at each other. As soon as the new customer sits, he orders whiskey. The daughter offers beer or wine.

"Whiskey."

The daughter offers beer or wine.

"No whiskey?"

"We serve beer or wine."

"How much is your beer? What kind?"

The mother heads for the kitchen.

The new customer orders two beers: "Both now."

He drinks one, then holds up the glass to complain. "Beer glasses should be kept in a freezer. You could put them in a freezer. In a classy place, glasses are kept in freezers. You can buy whiskey in the store?"

"No," the daughter says, "you can buy beer and wine."

"Not your store. I mean a *store*."

The daughter starts to explain Virginia state liquor laws, then stops. "You can buy beer and wine here—with your meal."

The father comes from the kitchen, leans behind the counter. The customer sees him, starts to say something, then rolls his head, stretching his neck till it cracks. He adjusts his shoulders before he speaks. "A meat sandwich, OK? Beer."

The customer has bricklayer shoulders. His hair isn't long, but needs a cut. There's mud on the sleeves of his shirt and in his hair. The shirt is sturdy fancy, silver snaps on the cuffs and pockets. The snaps look like rivets. One side of the man's hair looks bleached. He wears good stitched cowboy boots. No mud on the boots, but they're wet.

The daughter places two full glasses on the table. He tells her wait, stabs at the newspaper he's brought in, a local filled with ads.

"People just want to sell you stuff. Crip-Crap. Shit." He folds the paper. "Camper tops. Tarps." He slaps an ad with his hand: "Some jack wants to sell bayonets."

The customer looks at the daughter like she's the last person on earth. It is not a look of longing, but of grief. Then as though he's been pushed under water, he stretches his head up, sucks a breath. The mother delivers the food, escorts her daughter to behind the counter.

The cowboy bolts his sandwich, gulps beer, then argues about his ticket. He says to the daughter, before figuring, twice, his bill: "Had an apple. Put it on the table. Everybody just passes by." The daughter looks over to her father who, since before the food was served, has stayed behind the counter. It was the mother who finished preparing the meal.

When the cowboy asks to see a menu, it is the father who carries one over. The cowboy stares at it. On his way to pay, he makes a point of passing my table, which he jars with his hip. I have to make a grab for my beer.

The cowboy pushes money over the counter, then for all of his fuss, doesn't wait for change. Though he'd worn no coat in from outdoors, he stops at his table as if to seek one. By the time he reaches the restaurant door, the father is there with it open.

The draft from the door feels real. The father stops, asks if everything is OK, then returns to whatever he has been doing in the kitchen. Unbidden, the daughter brings a second beer, then sets up what looks like homework at one of the tables. She pushes the tableware and condiments out of her way. The mother, at the counter, is making a list.

Barrie would have named the customer, then made a list too:

1. *His mother assigned the father's name: Richard.*
2. *Which Richard changes to Rick.*
3. *Rick / Richard gets fired about once a week.*
4. *Poor Richard hasn't a coat.*
5. *He leaves tools out (in the rain).*
6. *Every time he's canned, he's confused.*
7. *But: Richard is dirty handsome, could star in a movie where he squints.*
8. *Hands. Arms. Chest hair. Trucks. Squints.*
9. *A movie about trucks, starring Rick.*

Richard would pay and leave, but Barrie wouldn't watch him. The door would slam. "Poor Richard has no coat."

In the morning, Richard's face is front-page. Except his name is Coles—Robert Coles—and he's dead. But before he dies (before he dines in Herndon) Coles manages to shoot a federal agent in a parking lot in D.C.

Coles has killed before. He'd read a newspaper account of some killers in Ogden, Utah, who strode into a music store, bound the Mormon family owners, punched their eardrums with wire, forced them to drink lye, then duct-taped their lips.

The day after he reads the story, Coles begins to track and fire at armored trucks. He writes to his aunt about the murderers in Utah and about himself and the armored trucks. In his letter, now transcribed in the *Post*, he promises he will fire only at bullet-proof trucks. *The glass in those trucks don't crack. The brains who invented those trucks learned about good glass from space. You shoot rocketships like bullets, right? You ever hear about rocketship windows cracking?*

Coles's spree carries him from Decatur, Illinois, ninety-one miles to Terre Haute (he keeps a log they find in his pickup: meals, gas, miles, motels) through Indiana into Ohio. He shoots four bullets, four trucks. Then outside Cleveland at a rest stop, he nails a guard who opens the truck door just as Bob fires his 30.30 from a prone position from atop a bluff.

Coles motors through to Pennsylvania, where he hopes to find, he writes to his aunt, different work. He mails her cards from locations where he stops.

Dear Pearl—
    Pennsylvania is forever acrossed so I'm sure to find work. I slugged some queers in Bath. Jim Thorpe is a town. So is Trappe. And a town called The King of Prussia. I'm in Bath.
    Then:
    Larry Holmes was born in Easton, Penn. He is the boxing champion of our world. I could ask him to write LARRY HOLMES on a glove.

And:

I will write again. I am your sister's son. I am going to Quakertown to mail my next card. I have been looking on the map.

Coles's aunt delivers Coles's letters to the state police, who deliver them to the FBI. When the Feds corner Coles, it's in D.C., on the night of the ice storm. Coles kills one agent, disables the other, after which he escapes to Herndon, where he eats supper with me and the Greeks.

Service stations closed by weather, Coles maneuvers his pickup on empty over ice, bearing west. Then, probably without so much as shifting in his seat, crushes the accelerator to the floor, plows from a hard curve into a farmer's yard. You can see the red pickup cough, spin, then jump from the road.

The farmer's yard harbors a dozen ancient mobile homes. "Gypsy trailers, really," says Virgil Mund, owner. It's all on TV, early local news.

"That one there," Virgil points with an orthopedic hook, "belonged to my father. He come here to Virginia to lease, but he bought this farm."

The trailer Mund means is a cartoon teardrop on its side—it might sleep two people. All the trailers are this size, feature rotted tires. Virgil moves to a boxy one, bangs it with his claw. "This here's the only one bought new." Painted on this trailer's back is V. MUND above a rising bass, blue aluminum lakes. Virgil strides through the debris, kicks at Coles's pickup, which is on its cab, wheels up. All the window glass is spidered.

"He was humping for my porch. I was out for a smoke and a watch on the storm. Trailers saved me." Mund readjusts his cap, then removes it to have something in his hand. He snaps the bill with the split metal of his hook.

Then a panoramic shot: the trailers, the porch, Coles's truck, the iced creek, the stiff unseeded fields. The interview, taped at sunrise, is bright, even on TV. The crystal surface of the earth mirrors sun. The violence of Coles's overturned pickup—the scattered trailers—has cracked ice, which bombards with white light, like broken jars.

I wish to be in Virgil's fields rather than in this rented room behind drapes. Were I to stand in Mund's fields, I would smell no spilled gas. Coles would not have sensed the irony. He would have pushed the pedal to the floor and there would have been just enough fuel to kill him.

The camera cuts to the nearest field. A lone cow stands beside a solitary oak (*genus* Quercus *of the* Beech *family, found in north temperate zones and Polynesia*). You can track the cow's path over the ice to the oak. Sun jumps from the ice. All is quiet.

By noon, with the hotel's help, I have rented a Chevette. I sign up for all the insurance, though the roads are now clear. The ribbon asphalt steams, but the road shoulders shine.

I drive the numbered highway, named and mapped on TV, to Virgil Mund's, a secondary road to Manassas. I know from the rental agency's map I'm in *Civil War Country: The Battles of Bull Run*. And: a bit north, also on the map, just across Maryland's border, *Antietam*, where September 17, 1862, General George Brinton McClellan struck the Confederate Army. On that day, McClellan lost 12,410 men, Lee 13,724. According to the Civil War notes, General McClellan and his Army of the Potomac were winners.

When I pass a sign pointing to a cutoff to Manassas National Battlefield Park, I stop to check my route. The Mund farm has to be near here, where in August 1862, per the map notes, the South managed to "rout" the North. *This* day, three weeks before Antietam, was Lee's. He lost but 9,197 troops, the Federal commander, 16,054.

I take the time to do the math to check the accuracy of the notes. Antietam *is* the bloodiest single day of war. Antietam defeats the second Battle of Bull Run by 883 perished. *Perished? or just casualties?* I hear Barrie say. *I mean, shouldn't there be a formula, one weighting for real deaths, others for degrees of damage—eye, mind, thumb, toe, ball, knee, bicep? Except it doesn't matter—Antietam is the victor, hands down. The second Bull Run was a two-day deal.*

I look up and down the road, then accelerate again toward Manassas. There are no troops or movement, and I'm the only car on the road. Then I see it. Within musket range of Manassas Creek—*Bull Run*—is Mund's farm. His painted name on the mailbox flames phosphorescent, even in full sun. The mailbox and driveway intersect the apex of the highway's curve.

I park beside the Mund name so as to not block the gravel drive to the house. When I park on the shoulder, the weight of the car cracks the ice. I open the door and inch forward. It sounds as though I'm crushing beetles or teeth. I prop the door open with my foot to listen, pull farther off than I mean and nearly slide on into the ditch which separates the highway from Virgil's fields.

In the ditch are long frozen ruts. Dungarees have been laid in the ruts for traction. The work pants seem part of the earth, as natural and adamant as the mud. There are un-iced heel marks in the ditch, as brush has sheltered it from the storm. On up, in another set of ruts, is a black snake. Or husk. Crows have worked him. The mud prints of the crows' feet look like busy fossils.

Beyond the ditch a fence section is down. Beyond that are the scattered trailers, the iced tree, fields. There is movement in the house as I move on the gravel to Virgil's porch. Virgil pushes through his door, ball cap on his head, belted work pants, an unbuttoned coat. He walks to the edge of his porch as if it were the end of both our worlds. The left cuff of his coat is ripped. His shirtsleeve shows through the rip like paint. From the right cuff, the hook swings.

I tell Virgil my name, that I'd seen him on TV, that I'd seen Coles in Herndon before he drove his pickup here. I point to the wreckage of trailers. Virgil sizes me up. "Mund," he says, without extending his hook or hand, then moves to the stairs of his unrailed porch to sit at the top of his steps. I sit too. We sit together, estimate ice and sun and soil. Oxygen, processing in my chest, feels bright.

Coles's pickup is gone. The cow too. But the trailers still lie, assaulted. Vapors rise like battle smoke from the creek. Virgil offers to make cigarettes, digs for fixings. When I decline the cigarette, Virgil smokes it.

When I inquire about the ditch, Virgil says, yes, they are his pants. Fools are always in his ditch. "A curve stays a curve—you know?" He smokes his cigarette as though it were a roach, clipping it delicately with his hook. He thrusts his chin at the hook: "Dog," lifts both shoulders then drops them, then removes his upper plate, which he rotates in the sun.

Virgil, it seems, doesn't feel his mouth collapse. He talks, holding his upper teeth in front like a mirror. In the presence of that face, the extracted teeth, the hook, the trailers, I feel what seems like the existence of ghosts. If Virgil feels ghosts, the look he turns towards me in broad daylight tells me he doesn't mean to discuss it. Virgil does not, for a minute, though, look from me.

Virgil reaches to place his teeth on the porch between us, then doesn't. He opens his mouth for the teeth, shoves them in like a tape cassette, then constructs a second smoke, his good left hand a machine. The pouch and the paper in the hand look puny. The product which emerges seems the consequence of a spell. The cigarette is perfect. Even Virgil seems pleased. He plucks it up with his hook, lights up.

"Dog bite poisoned the hand. Mama put a poultice on it. Didn't take. Ever use a poultice?" Virgil presents his hook with its butt to the sun. Virgil considers his own question, then scissors the butt to the ground.

A thirty-year-old Nash Rambler sails, two toned, into the curve. The woman, who you can see has bleached her hair, lays on the horn. She slows and waves, blasts the horn, fires around the bend. Virgil raises his hook, too late. He studies the place where the old coupe has just passed. "I should clear them trailers before the ground melts muck."

Then: "Can't think of the name. Can't remember the old girl's name. Won't be long till it's muck." Then: "I fucked her. Can't remember the name."

When I turn to Virgil, he's propelling smoke toward the horizon. I set a hand on his shoulder because I want to touch someone. If he notices, he doesn't mind. Then I walk the cow's visible path to the nearest huge tree, which, still shelled in ice, appears cold and black and holy. Then beyond, I stand at the fence, alone. From here the fields stretch improbably, unburdened by anything but ice and promise. Without my help, sun is melting Mund's fields.

sab·o·tage

A 1918 dictionary lists smashing machines, flooding mines, burning wheat, ravaging fruit and provisions, blowing reservoirs and aqueducts, wrecking track, etc., as acts of *sabotage*. In 1931, the *Observer* reported that two managers of a dairy were dubbed *saboteurs* and sentenced to five and two years' imprisonment for permitting two hundred tons of butter to spoil.

Sabot, the French word for wooden shoe, appears as a word in English as early as 1607. According to the OED, it then meant in English what it meant in French: a shoe made from a single piece of wood shaped and hollowed out to fit the foot. But imagining the sound of folk clonking in wooden shoes allows, sometime later, for this: *sabotage,* "to make a noise with sabots, to perform or execute badly, e.g. to 'murder' (a piece of music)." Or, perhaps more benignly: a noisy bungling of things, a "botching."

Traditionally, however, *sabotage* is associated with workers throwing wooden shoes into machines with intent to damage machines. As a word, *sabotage* first appears in English around 1910, gaining special currency during World War I. Some connect the word with the Great French Railway Strike of 1912, though detractors point out that wooden shoes were more often worn by peasants than by city-dwelling factory workers. The first instances of *sabotage* were likely, then, peasant revolts against oppressive landowners—a trampling of crops, a disabling of harvesting equipment.

In the *American Heritage Dictionary,* "sabotage" is found on the same page, in the same column as "*saber-toothed tiger*" and "*SAC,*" the acronym of the Strategic Air Command, the step-brainchild of General Curtis E. LeMay. Long before he hooked up with George C. Wallace as the vice-presidential candidate on the 1968 American Independent third-party-*Bomb-'em-back-to-the-Stone-Age*-ticket, LeMay (in 1945, the youngest major general in the Army Air Corps) took over the Twenty-First Bomber Command in the Mariana Islands.

The naval victory in the Battle of the Philippine Sea cleared the island decks for LeMay. From his new post, LeMay inaugurated low-level bombing tactics that burned fifty-nine Japanese cities. In five months, LeMay orchestrated enough civilian casualties in Japan to double those of the Japanese military worldwide in forty-five months of fighting. The tightly packed wooden cities of Japan proved incendiaries in particular effective.

Discovered by Ferdinand Magellan in 1521, the Marianas, a series of volcanic and coral formations, were renamed by Jesuit missionaries to honor Mariana of Austria, regent of Spain in the late 1600s. The islands had been before known as "Ladrones"—that is, "Thieves" Islands.

Early in his autobiography, *Mission with LeMay: My Story,* LeMay recounts the story of his being hired, at age nine, to shoo

English sparrows for a neighbor to feed her cat—a cat too infirm to hunt on its own.

The rifle actually didn't belong to me. It was a beat-up single-shot .22 which was brought into the crowd of neighborhood little boys by some other fellow, and kind of shared by all of us. The proceeds had to be shared too, and I considered this an imposition. I did the shooting and paid for my ammunition, but still I had to divvy up a certain proportion of my spoils. This was because I didn't own the rifle involved. It was a pretty good lesson too. Everybody ought to have his own weapons and not depend on others to furnish them.

Unlike boys who might be eager to shoot a bird until they shoot one, young LeMay's production stayed well ahead of the old cat's needs.

Only trouble was, the cat's appetite couldn't quite keep up with my willingness and ability to supply the English sparrows. A lot of the time I had to sit around and cool my heels, waiting for Puss to get hungry again. I resolved that I must acquire a .22 of my own, just as soon as humanly possible. Did, too.

By 1945, LeMay had acquired plenty. Planning to attack Tokyo, he reconfigured his B-29s for increased numbers of bombs—fire-bombs—then modified bombing altitudes, patterns.

Here's what happened. We ordered three hundred and twenty five planes to that job, and eighty-six percent of them attacked the primary target. We lost just four-and-three-tenths percent of all the B-29s which were airborne. Sixteen hundred and sixty-five tons of incendiary bombs went hissing down upon that city, and hot drafts from the resulting furnace tossed some of our aircraft two thousand feet above their original altitude. We burned up nearly sixteen square miles of Tokyo.

General Thomas "Tommy" Power, who flew the lead aircraft:

It was the greatest single disaster incurred by any enemy in military history. It was greater than the combined damage of Hiroshima and Nagasaki. There were more casualties than in any other military action in the history of the world.

Tokyo was struck twice. A total of 1,022 aircraft dropped some seven thousand tons of bombs. With 50.8 percent of the city reduced to ashes, Tokyo was removed from the list of incendiary targets.

To be fair, 1945 was a year of excessive rainfall and floods in Japan. In some cases, earthquakes destroyed homes, but by the end of five months of firebombing, a quarter of the houses in Japan were gone. Put another way, twenty-two million people were homeless.

Japanese leadership had ordered children evacuated from the cities. At the same time, all men and women fifteen and older were ordered to enroll in the militia. With a "defense" force of fifty million, the Japanese ruling clique hoped to make the Americans think twice about invasion. A by-product was to make American air raids on Japanese cities a "legitimate" act of war, as the cities were now "military installations." U.S. incendiaries burned the wooden and paper Japanese cities like willing tinder, inducing firestorms that melted people.

Within an hour of the first firestorm (the RAF raid on Hamburg, Germany, 28 July 1943), the Hamburg Fire Department recorded the incident by coining the word *Feuersturm* to describe it.

When many buildings are ablaze, great heat is generated and the convection the fires cause not only sucks in air but disseminates sparks and burning debris to start other conflagrations. The more fires, the greater the heat and convection until, in seconds, all fires coalesce. Hurricane winds are then created, ingesting oxygen and promoting temperatures. At two thousand degree Fahrenheit, water and blood boil.

LeMay's arrival in the Marianas to prepare the bomber command to attack Japan is noted in his autobiography as private musings:

... *On-the-job training. We've got to do that ...*

Let's see: where can we find some Japs to practice on, someone within our range? Away down below, in Burma, there must be a few Japs ... some of those ports down there. Maybe we could even go as far as Singapore.

Later:

. . . Intelligence says that every one of those factories is surrounded by a hundred-foot firebreak. But if we really got rolling with incendiaries, and had a wind to help us with the flames, firebreaks wouldn't make any difference . . . Ninety per cent of the structures made of wood. By golly, I believe that Intelligence report said ninety-five! And what do they call that other kind of cardboard stuff they use? Shoji. *That's it.*

After Nagoya and Osaka, LeMay concluded *"that the Toyko raid had not been a fluke."*

Following the initial ten days of firebombing, General LeMay thought *that a man might have the right to some sort of mild celebration.* He sends for cigars. *I craved a celebration, and I was going to celebrate with Havanas or know the reason why.*

Following the March 1945 fire blitz, LeMay ran out of ammunition and had to stall four weeks for the next incendiary attacks. It must have proved a hard wait, as after a month of firebombing, the skies above Japan were so safe that it was actually safer to fly a combat mission over Japan than to fly a B-29 training mission in the United States. By this light, combat aircraft dumped all their guns and cannons in order to carry more bombs.

When it came time for the atomic bomb, Toyko was removed from the list.

. . . we had to have a fresh target—at least a target whereon no great destructive capacity had yet been exerted. None of the burned-up towns would do. Tokyo wouldn't do. There would be no possible way to measure the new bomb's effectiveness against a landscape of cinders.

So it was a problem of sorts to select two cities for "Little Boy" and "Fat Man." *By the time the nuclear strikes were launched against Hiroshima and Nagasaki, we were running out of major targets.*

Although the atomic-bomb sorties were carried out from the Marianas, LeMay hadn't been involved with the scheme. He was, just before, informed by way of a personal letter from President

Truman. *Let me say this,* LeMay said after, *it was one of the best-kept military secrets of the war.*

Then:

Uranium, plutonium; "Little Boy, Fat Man": the world knows those weapons now, every school child knows. No use describing the mushroom-shaped column, the unbelievable light, and weird color of the flash and resulting clouds . . . unearthly debris and steaming destruction and massive death. It's an old and familiar story now, from Bikini on. These bombs brought into the world not only their own speed and extent of desolation. They brought a strange pervading fear which does not seem to have affected mankind previously, from any other source. This unmitigated terror has no justice, no basis in fact. Nothing new about death, nothing new about deaths caused militarily. We scorched and boiled and baked to death more people in Tokyo on that night of March 9–10 than went up in vapor at Hiroshima and Nagasaki combined.

And:

I have indeed bombed a number of specific targets. They were military targets on which the attack was, in my opinion, justified morally. I've tried to stay away from hospitals, prison camps, orphan asylums, nunneries and dog kennels. I have sought to slaughter as few civilians as possible.

Interred at the United States Air Force Academy Cemetery, Colorado, LeMay lies in Area 3, Row D, Number 77. Should you visit, the gravesite is near the flagpole and, like its neighbors, denoted by an unobtrusive bas-relief brass plaque measuring twelve inches by twenty-four inches (actually 23¾ inches, ⅛ inch shaved from each end to make the plaque's length just shy of two feet). The brass plaque lies flat to the surface of the earth, a touch below the plane of grass.

As suggested by a survey of a number of modern dictionaries sab·o·tage means interference with production, work, etc., under mining a cause, etc., injuring or attacking, instilling terror, etc

Consider a definition (number 3, say) for *saboteur*. 3. LeMay, Curtis E. (Emerson). See Japan, 1945.

As students of these things know, the bombing of Japan was an attempt to avoid an amphibious landing. Projected casualty figures were the product of the American experience on Saipan and Okinawa. Using the "Saipan ratio," some staffers predicted two million U.S. casualties. This figure began to move downward, until by the spring of 1945, the number five hundred thousand was more often quoted. In any event, the U.S. Army ordered the production of four hundred thousand Purple Hearts.

It must be said that low-level, saturation firebombing of Japan's wood-and-paper cities pushed Japan toward surrender. A common denominator for the burned cities is that they were congested and flammable.

"I'll tell you what war is about," LeMay said after. *"You've got to kill people, and when you've killed enough they stop fighting."*

General John Chain (in 1990 the SAC commander and presiding at LeMay's full-honors funeral) said of his mentor: *"He was tough, but tough in a compassionate way."*

LeMay couldn't smile. A botched sinus operation prevented him from curving his lips.

There's nothing new about this massacre of civilian populations. In ancient times, when an army laid siege to a city, everybody was in the fight. And when that city had fallen, and was sacked, just as often as not every single soul was murdered.

The American Boeing B-29 Superfortress heavy bomber is powered by four Wright R-3350-23 Cyclone radials, 2,200-hp each. It is capable of speeds of up to 365 mph at 25,000 feet. Its range is 5,380 miles maximum. With its normal armament of up to twelve half-inch Browning machine guns and one 20-mm cannon, it can carry 20,000 lbs of bombs. Without guns and cannon, and flying low level, more.

The now aging B-52 Stratofortress entered the inventory during LeMay's tenure as SAC commander. A fully armed single

B-52, as it lifts skyward, becomes the fourth most powerful armed force in the world. Between 1954 and 1962, 744 B-52s were built—some ninety remain in service.

The climate of the Marianas is tropical and the economy largely agricultural, with dependence on the harvesting of copra, the dried white flesh of coconut, from which coconut oil can be extracted, then used to scent shampoo, sunscreen, candles . . .

1 October 1990: Curtis LeMay dies in a military hospital in California, six weeks short of his eighty-fourth birthday. It takes three days to prepare and deliver the remains to Colorado. As the casket arrives, SAC bombers fly overhead and two hundred Air Force Academy cadets stand at attention. Consider that forty-five years have passed since the Marianas forays into Japan. Consider the unmolested blue skies of Colorado. Consider SAC's improved capacities, though for the burial flyby nary a pamphlet is dropped, nor iron, nor fire, nor steel, nor shoes. Consider a pair of plain sabots atop LeMay's conforming brass plaque, burning.

Accident

I'd started junior high before my father stood
at full height to box me. Before that, he kneeled on folded ore
bags, canvas sacking he'd brought home from the mines. He used
the same two bags to stow the gloves. They were pillow gloves,
maybe twenty-ouncers.

My father could have tagged me at will, but what he did was
tap at me and root me on to slug him. "Belt me," he'd say. "Go
on." I once managed to sneak through his guard to bloody his
nose. The bloom on his face shocked me. My father tapped back
before he tilted his head to walk to the sink. I stowed the boxing
gloves in the ore bags for him. I was twelve years old.

When my father was a boy, he worked like a man to support his family: father, mother, sister. My father's father was a boxer and a gambler and a drunk. My father adored him. When my grandfather died, my father said to me, "You knew him as a drunk, but he was a god. You don't know. I should know."

By the time he was twelve, it was three years into the Great Depression. Tall for his age, my father was driving a truck in Butte, Montana, hawking firewood door to door. He sold the wood he'd helped his father cut. Most of my father's wood customers were unemployed. If people had money at all, he said, they were converting to coal.

My grandfather had rigged up a false-bottomed truck, so that when my father sold a "cord" of wood, he had to stack it so it wouldn't look short. "How you do that?" I asked, because we burned wood at our house and because I helped him to split the wood and to stack it. "Show me."

"No."

My father was not encouraged to attend school from the sixth grade on. "I was tired all the time and ashamed of my clothes. I wouldn't be a kid again for nothing." My father finished high school and managed even—supporting his own new family as well as his mother and father—to complete two years at the Montana School of Mines. His dream had been to be a metallurgical engineer, the science of procedures to extract precious metals from ore. "Fancy sluicing," my father said, "that's all."

When I was admitted into a graduate English program, my father offered his briefcase. The year I'd started high school, my father quit the mines for six months to try his hand at sales, but he couldn't sell enough asphalt seal to equal what he made in the mines so was forced back underground. The briefcase he'd used for his failed sales was the one he gave me to use. When I completed my degree, my father asked for the briefcase. I emptied it, handed it over. "It was just a lend," he said. I don't now remember the name of the sealant my father had sold, but the word "Texas" was in it. He'd had the words tooled into the side of the briefcase.

My father was bewildered by my choice of English. Not that he didn't respect the art of literature, he said. He could repeat from memory long sections of "Hiawatha" or "The Courtship of Miles

Standish," and the full texts of poems like "The Village Black-smith" and "The Cremation of Sam McGee."

And he invented bedtime stories, serials he recounted about Indian boys, eagles, Eskimos, bears, gold fields, the Nez Perce, the Royal Canadian Mounted Police. There were dogs in most of his stories. I remember, in particular, a story about an enchanted Hereford bull. In this story, my father invents a displaced prince who is saved by a magic bull. Large as a shed, the animal runs like the wind and talks. And: whenever Jack the Prince is hungry, he unscrews the bull's horn: a cornucopia filled with food and drink. In the story, too, is a dragon, a wicked Queen stepmother, a wicked bull, a weak King, a comely princess, a bigheaded and loyal dog, and a jaunty crew of royal cowboys. The story ran on for weeks. My friends came to hear my father's inventions, as my father's pals had tagged home with him to the wood yard to watch my grandfather manhandle logs, then hand saw them. "Arms like a god," my father reported.

When I graduated from high school, my father handed me his Faber slide rule and Dietzgen drafting set. For years he had worked to laud math and the convenience of the slide rule in my presence. He touted the profits of Powers and Hyperbolic Logarithms and Roots. Like poems, he could recite the rules and functions he'd put to memory from trigonometry and his college calculus years before.

On the one-month anniversary of my father's death at seventy-three, I called home. My mother was out, so my father answered the phone. During his forty years in smelters and mines in Utah and Montana, and even after he'd retired, my father had run a landscaping business for extra income from out of the home. His voice on the answering machine, he said, "I can't come to the phone now, but if you'll leave your name and number and the time you called. . . . " I phoned back to hear the recording.

On the third Sunday following my father's death, I drove to SAFEWAY for mozzarella for pizza. I'd started to try to do normal things, like cooking, but in the grocery—this place of reason and set exchange: everything priced—other patrons seemed to be shopping without event. For a time, I stood and watched the shoppers shop (Sprite, Lean Cuisine, COLORADO SCRATCH LOTTO— *Ace in the Hole, High Roller, Barrel of Bucks, Score*—cigarettes COORS), then found the cheese, SAFEWAY's own brand: shredded milk in resealable plastic. Heading for the registers, I came face to face with a display of WELLS LAMONT work gloves. There they were: the HANDYANDYS, the Mules, the TUFF-GUYS, the Grippers. I burst into tears. There was no helping this. I might as well have ordered my stomach valves to swing open or shut, the sponge or the press of my kidneys. I escaped SAFEWAY, but on my way out what I craved was for someone to stop me long enough to ask what was wrong—for when this occurred, I meant to injure the person. I meant to administer a blow.

At the mortuary I'd felt this way. I disliked the funeral director even before he pitched his script. I disliked his using my mother's first name. Now he rose for the showroom tour. All the time he'd been speaking, his back had been to the casket showroom: a scald-ingly lit room behind uncurtained glass. Because we faced the director, we had faced the room. It was a lot like watching welding.

Although up and ready, backing towards the overlit room, the director was dodging the topic of burial cost by discussing coffin accouterments: gaskets, liners, weather stripping, ornament finish. *Equipage,* he actually said. I wanted to lay an arm about the director's taller shoulders to whisper, smiling, something raw in his ear. What I did was ask the director to please, if he would, excuse us. "Oh my," he said. "Of course," he said, then rushed from the room.

My youngest brother and I stayed at the mortuary while my mother rode home with my sisters. I'd asked my mother to en-trust my brother and me with selecting the coffin. My brother and I had just closed the showroom door when the director reap-peared. I shot him a look through the glass. Without turning about, he slid off. He seemed to be gliding on ball bearings.

The coffins had names, like resort condos: *Sequoia, Sierra Cascade.* Without warning, I was struck with the notion that was not where I was, but in a Soapbox-Derby or dog-sled store— basic frames for the buyer's sequent choice of spoked wheels or steel runners. I could have been standing in an outlet for damaged goods: coffee tables, say, with warped tops, or half-assed trunks or single-bed waterbed bargains. Everything—in a room of one-size-fits-all—seemed the designed consequence of shoddy work. Or accident: *spot-lit accident*.

You live long enough to learn every accident is not unfortunate. It was accident that kept my father from war. In 1940, he'd wanted to enlist in the Navy. He and a pal meant to sign up so long as they could be promised the same ship. They both signed, but after a physical, my father was refused enlistment because of a damaged eye—a childhood mishap (a flying wood chip) in my grandfather's wood yard. My father's pal died aboard ship at Pearl Harbor. My father married three years later: New Year's Day, 1944.

Now, three weeks shy of the fiftieth marking of this day, my brother and I were deciding on our father's coffin. We selected wood. My father had taught us professional tree work: to prune a tree, to top a tree, to remove one. When we removed trees, he would remark on the grain and pattern of stumps, compute a tree's age, further studying rings to disclose for us hard winters, unadvertised disease, and other untoward, now revealed, hurt. My brother and I chose a dark-grained box.

I was a freshman in high school—1961—when Gary Cooper, my father's movie hero, died. *Felled*, the man who'd been, my father said, *Marco Polo, Lou Gehrig, Sergeant York*. My father had told me about Alvin York. A basic story of good and evil, told in simple and profound terms, was how I heard it: a conscientious objector who could shoot. Alvin York, the pacifist crack-shot, kills twenty Germans and captures one hundred thirty-two others—the largest bagging of prisoners by a single soldier in the recorded history of war. York's flanking and destruction of the German machine-gun nests had saved thousands. Ever the averse hero, York had killed to stop the killing, he said. Cooper won an Oscar for the 1941 role.

Eleven years later, Gary Cooper was awarded a second Oscar for his role as Will Kane, the cowboy marshal of *High Noon*. I was six years old when this, "the first adult Western," was shot, so it was later that my father explained it: on the day of his retirement from the law and his marriage to a Quaker girl, Cooper, as Kane, controls his fear and waits for four outlaws who are coming to town to kill him. In a fit of panic, Cooper had been fleeing with his new bride. My father then related how Cooper, of a sudden, pulls up. There is a shot of Cooper in the buckboard with Grace Kelly. The horse stills and the dust settles in the open prairie. "I've got to go back," Cooper says, then turns the buckboard towards town.

No longer officially the law and under no sensible person's moral obligation, Cooper returns to defend the town and the rightness of his having put the honcho outlaw into prison years before. Let down by townsfolk and friends, Cooper alone faces the bully outlaw and his murderous crew. Not lost on my father is that Grace Kelly, Cooper's Quaker wife, fires a bullet just in time to kill one of the outlaws to save her new husband's life. Also not lost is that Cooper, business finished, drops his tin star in the dirt. I've learned that Cooper had been ill throughout the thirty-one days of the filming of *High Noon*, which was why he'd looked so convincingly haggard and drawn. It was this natural appearance on screen that as much as anything helped Cooper collect his second Academy Award.

In any case, Frank James ("Gary") Cooper—my father's senior by nineteen years—had been born in Helena, Montana, less than an hour's drive from Butte, where my father'd been raised, been wed, and his own children had been born. Gary Cooper, my father's immortal, died at sixty, an unlucky thirteen years sooner than my own father at seventy-three.

When my father died, I wrote two friends. One wrote back,

I was your age when my own father died, and my reaction must have been similar to your own. I went through the rituals of it—the funeral home, the greeting of visitors, the burial, the postburial Jewish gathering of mourners who had to be fed as they wept. I was shepherding my children as well as my own emotions and went through it all dry eyed. Then about two weeks later, alone with Carole in a restaurant, suddenly, like you, I began to weep. I no longer remember the cue, but doubt if it was as sensible as working gloves. Maybe the realization that so long as my father lived, I was still somebody's kid.

And the other, whose father had died two years before,

It is the time afterward that is toughest. You are hit unexpectedly by grief, with all defenses down. Suddenly you see someone who looks like your father, or someone about the same age, or you see something he would have liked, or hear someone say something he might have, and you are hit by his absence, by the fact that you can't ask him something only he would know.

I once called my father to have him walk me through on the phone the downing of a diseased elm beside my home. I knew how to remove the tree, had felled numbers of such trees with him. I'd phoned because I'd wanted my father to walk me through it, because I'd wanted him to know I was downing a tree, because I'd wanted him to know I knew who knew what to do.

"Notch it high so when you back-cut you'll be standing, not kneeling. You want to be able to move when a tree falls. Back-cut parallel to the notch, but higher—six . . . eight inches up—that way, the tree'll fall slow. But," he said, "you know that." He told me to call him later. "Let me know."

I arrived in Montana after my father had been removed from the hospital, so the first I saw him was at the wake. In his coffin, he looked as tall to me as he had when I was a boy, and as large handed. I've been both a son and a father long enough to know about the reciprocal failures of parents and children, and I didn't have to wait for my father to die to know I loved him, or he me. The wake was no tallying up, but there was this: in his coffin, my father looked resourceless. Impounded. Ungloved. He looked too heavy to lift.

My mother'd been pleased my father's hands had been crossed

in such a way that the right covered the left, which had been bruised by needles in the ICU, a thing she told me recently on the phone. During this call, I asked if Dad actually read things I'd published and sent home. "Oh, his one eye always bothered him," she said. I told Mom I'd called earlier, that Dad had answered the phone, that his voice was on the machine. "I know, but I'm going to wait," she said. "I'm waiting."

Ungiven to work, my father's father preferred to play cards, drink, box. He'd show at one of the mines in Butte on paydays, between shifts, to challenge all comers: *winner-take-all*. An opponent would be picked or come forth, someone would pass a hat, and, generally, my grandfather would sally home with the hat and the cash.

During the thirties, Dixie LaHood visited Butte, where my grandfather boxed him. Kid Dixie was a local, but also, at the time, a regarded regional tough who'd held his own against name fighters in San Francisco, Reno, Ogden, Salt Lake. He'd had a spot, my father claimed, on the fight card in Shelby, Montana, the day Jack Dempsey managed finally to control an impertinent Tommy Gibbons.

My grandfather and LaHood were light heavies. In a ring in the City Civic Center, my grandfather stepped through the ropes in his work shoes and stripped off his shirt. He wore long pants and a belt. Gloved up, he took more than he gave, then one-eyed—one eye punched shut—rared back and jockeyed a right that knocked Kid Dixie LaHood senseless. In the center of the Depression, my grandfather stepped out of the ring, bare chested, took his shirt and earnings, then walked home with my father, his son. How many chances like that does a father have?

The year I was twelve—the year I bloodied his nose—I accompanied my father to the mine on weekends. Saturdays, he and his crew worked half-days above ground to write up their reports. Dad and I'd pack lunches and head for the Lexington together. One Friday night, my father talked about this mining engineer who, coming off shift, had taken to sitting in the sampling office at my father's desk. My father was head sampler at the Lexington mine, boss of a day crew that collected ore for assaying. As I understood it, the mining engineer and his night crew, on their way to the showers, would track up the sampling office in the mornings before my father and his day crew arrived. The engineer had gone so far as to prop his grimed boots on the top of my father's desk.

The engineer was a good-sized man, I heard my father tell my mother. I heard him tell her, too, that he'd told the engineer if he caught him in his chair with his boots up, he'd knock him right to the floor. My father had announced this in front of both crews. I understood that the beef was about the two crews—the *samplers* and *engineers*, the *day* and *night* crews—though I understood, too, that if the drama played out, it would play out between only two from the crews: my father and the engineer.

My ears popped on the ascent in the car up the hill to the mine. We drove, then parked, then walked to my father's office. I sped ahead, saw the engineer first. He was tilted back in my father's castored chair, dirty boots on the desk. His back to us, he was laughing and talking. I stopped. My father's stride neither quickened nor slowed. He walked past me into the office, kicked the chair. The engineer crashed to the floor. He sprang up, almost tear eyed, but howling and ready. My father turned to his locker, extracted a set of red boxing gloves—*where had those come from?*—handed a pair to the engineer. These gloves were not twenty-ouncers. They looked like mittens you could wear ice fishing, though my father and the engineer donned them to box. In the mine yard, in front of two crews, my father conducted a clinic in fisticuffs.

That Saturday we left the Lexington before we ate lunch. We stopped at Clark Park. From here I could see the Civic Center, where my grandfather had decked Dixie LaHood, and I could see the hoist frame of the Lexington mine on the hill. My father and I sat on a bench and ate our lunches in the open air. An X ray was to show torn cartilage and cracked ribs, but he, head sampler, missed no work.

———————

Diagnosed with cancer, my father decided to refuse chemo, then died in less than a day: four heart attacks in fourteen hours. A real worker, waiting of any sort, for my father, if not unvirtuous, was no virtue. A few years back, following prostate surgery— one day out of the hospital—he climbed a tree to trim it. He fell from the tree, broke a leg.

What I know of my grandfather I know mostly from the stories my father told me. It's true I remember my father's father as a savaged drunk, but I should trust my father's stories as my son should trust mine, for when I die and take my memories of my grandfather's son, who will be left to love him?

I've not wanted to tell this story until I dreamed of my dead father. I'd written already what you've read about my father falling, after surgery, from a tree, and in dream he falls too, and it's the same tree, but instead of work gloves, he sports boxing mitts. In the dream, he grins, waves his oxblood fists. He speaks to me for the first time since the answering machine. I expect, "I can't come to the phone," but what he says is, "If you want to call me that, smile," Gary Cooper's response to Walter Huston in *The Virginian* after Huston calls him an SOB. I don't call my father a name, or by name, but I smile. For his part, he falls and falls, ready to break a leg. More often than not my father was in just such a rush, an accident waiting to happen.

Endnotes

1. Alsatians save him, the German General retells: set the bones, butter the face, lard the fists, then ship him to the Swiss who concoct *The Repair,* stripping the General's cracked legs for the flesh to do it.

2. Of the German High Command: "They were clever," *fehlerfreies Englisch* welling from the lattice of jaw (*jaw as trellis?*— i.e., draped trellis? swathed trellis? covered fretwork?). When the General bites on words, his teeth seem to fold.

3. Raps his breast where medals have hung.

4. Of credentials: nine hundred *Luftwaffe* missions for A. Hitler, thirty years NATO service, and a face enough disfigured by war to have become, quite thoroughly, a calling. The General

bobs his head, snaps his eyelids shut as he must have clamped them against the splash of the airplane fuel, then the flames.

5. "Bulked with tin."

6. The General (then Major) abandoned in the fireball of his plane forever his father-given face and hawk vision—his downing of so many Allied planes, he notes, more the agent of born eyesight than of machine or skill, single purpose, or luck.

7. "My chest paraded medals." Then: "When I entered Berlin, my city lay level."

8. The General lifts thumbless hands, then drops them. His eyes, in the focused light, look covered with coins, ruined copper.

9. "*Rubbled. . . .*"

10. A pretty professor stands, asks the guest to speak to the ace tactics employed to down over forty Allied pilots. She seems to have intentionally employed the term *pilots*, not *planes*.

10a. The General: "Decode, if you will, the two-day raid by two thousand Allied bombers igniting the city of Dresden?"

11. "In 1944, my uniform pressed, I traveled to Berlin. Females did truly regard me. I wore white laundered gloves."

12. "135,000."

13. The General extends his arms. In this stretch towards us, the General's jaw shuts, as though hinged to his wrists, the pole wrists.

14. "The target was of no military value."

15. With the slightest of shifts, the General's shoes catch the dais light. Even he looks down.

16. The medieval Dresden was the home of Europe's first china. In firing, the moisture in the clay is removed.

Epilogue

In the middle of the night, once, Barrie calls. "I'm reading obituaries since you."

"You weren't reading them before?"

"You don't read them?"

"Right after my father died, I started. You lose your DMZ, your math changes."

"DMZ?"

"Demilitarized Zone. *Buffer*. The math changes. Your sister would know."

"What?"

"Nothing."

"You read obits because you're aware or afraid?"

"You feel a difference?"

"Tell me."

"What?"

"You've been afraid?"

"I was fifteen, my father was transferred from the mines to the smelter and we moved to live in a company house. We had a pig when we lived in that house. *My father bought a pig.* It was hot. July. We had a fire hose—a company fire hose—piped up to the house. I opened it up, held on like a pro, nailed the pig, *killed* him."

"Killed?"

"Temperature? force? shock?—who knows? Pigs don't sweat, right?—can't sweat. I think I've heard that. I shut things down, rolled the hose, started overland to my father's office. Afraid? Hey."

"Most houses don't come with a fire hose."

"My whole life, I bit my nails. I'd chew right through the pepper polish my mother'd paint on. My father dies and I stop biting my nails. After forty years, I stop. One day I had nails to clip and file. I have them now. What's with that?"

In the East Wing, the first gallery Maryam and I come upon is space arranged for sculptor David Smith. Smith's steel boxes attach to one another, parallel to the axis of a main support, or perpendicular to it, or set at an angle to it. In the East Wing of the National Gallery of Art, on a winter night, with a princess, I see five of the thirty existing sets. I make pronouncements about order, simplicity, harmony, quoting a critic who in a printed note on the wall calls the glistening giants (some more than eight feet tall) "twentieth-century votive forms compatible with the age. In Smith, welded sculpture in America had its beginning *and* flowering, and in 'Cubi,' his finest assemblies." The critic next notes that two years into the series, Smith rammed his truck (loaded with steel) into a utility pole and death.

What for years had pleasured me in Henry Moore's ovate masses cowers under the spell of Smith's rectangular steel. And whatever violence had occurred in Smith's cutting and welding I feel advancing as calm.

Maryam: "Too much of nothing."

What had I expected? Who?—Barrie? Trace? *A beshined statement of elimination and paring?* "Sculpture occupies space in ways humans can't," Trace'd said. "You can stare at it."

Maryam: "All these blocks?"

"He ran the risk of repetition." I inform that Smith had trained as a hard-hat welder at an auto plant. "Studebaker," I say. I'd read it in the critic's note. "My father owned a Studebaker. Push-button transmission."

But Maryam prefers the polyvinyl sculpture of John DeAndras, whose work I'd first seen the day I'd met Trace. The life form had seemed more effective to me that day. But now with Maryam in the gallery adjacent to Smith's, I know I don't like the six nudes.

All the figures are female and naked. Maryam likes the artist's valuing of the ordinary, says so: "What is more ordinary than naked people?"

I remember a story about a crazed lady who'd stripped, then spray-painted herself gold. The reporter reported the woman had reported no reason, but what isn't clear? We all work to make ourselves appear valuable. Don't we? I repeat the story to Maryam. "Don't we?"

Maryam wonders why I appreciate the spray-painted woman but not DeAndras's six vinyl ones.

"Their skin seems crawly as mine. And hair—where'd he get the hair?"

"Samoa. No blondes here."

"Worse than clones," I say. "Phony clones."

Maryam says the revered Coleridge has been wrong in his notion of art as a suspension of disbelief. "Art's an agreed-upon pretense. What's with you? Is that Tennessee Williams? Isn't that the American playwright Williams?"

For no reason I can defend, I'm taken aback by foreigners who are well read. I look at DeAndras's work and argue about the women. "This is taxidermy. Husks. Morgue feet. The naked feet creep me. All they're missing are tags, IDs. Do you know how he makes these things? He takes actual body casts, then melts in his plastic, adds hair. Dolls' eyes. Nails. Pink paint. He makes a career of this, and it's a one-trick trick. The first time I saw his work, there was one figure—and I guess I thought that was it. By the way, I should say, she was a redhead." Then: "You know how Williams died? He choked to death. On the cap from a nasal spray."

Maryam says, "Americans imagine death is always to be averted if possible, but we are never choosing between life and death, only between death now or in a while. Americans are children."

I expect Maryam to make a case for this art she is saying she likes, compare it, say, to photography, but she doesn't. "These women," she says. She means the nudes. "What grandmother wouldn't want such a self to point to?"

"A vinyl nude in every carport." I go back to my argument about false clones. I say you also have to pass on guts and muscles and nerve roads. "Destinies, Maryam. Destinies."

The look Maryam projects I remember. I remember, too, what I'd written to Trace about the red-haired nude we'd seen together in Philadelphia: *Longer lasting than tin or bronze, the redhead will outlive me or you, but she'll do it without the pangs of doom, nostalgia, toil, alarm, fury, gesture, loss.* What I'd felt about that vinyl nude I realized was now the objection. Of course.

Appendix

Therapist: favorite word?

Mann: rainfall

Therapist: least favorite?

early

Therapist: what turns you on, excites, inspires?

Mondrian, Count Basie, Frank Lloyd Wright blueprints

Therapist: one answer

I said

Therapist: off? turns you off?

books made into movies

Therapist: a noise you enjoy?

Sinatra and Washington, Dinah Washington. You remember Brook Benton?

Therapist: dislike?

hailstones

Therapist: favorite curse word?

fuck—there are others . . .

Therapist: what profession other than yours do you seriously think you'd enjoy?

landscaper? Sure, that.

Therapist: dream profession?

Basie's drummer

Therapist: profession you would least enjoy?

security guard, computer salesman, blind man

Therapist: can you narrow it?

sure—eunuch. *Then*: All this sounds like something you might ask a celebrity on TV. I mean who gives a shit . . . favorite curse word? No, you know what this feels like?—not a real psychological test, more like a test a regular person might think was real. Look, I ran over my own dog. Tell you what, here's a dream: "Barrie reads from a book of stories by Diane Vreuls."

Therapist: Barrie? Vreuls?—who's Barrie?

she makes me pronounce it: "Say it: *Vreuls*. Dutch. Must be." Barrie's in a hospital, strapped in a bed, though her arms have been freed for reading. The story Barrie reads aloud has to do with the chance meeting of Vreuls's character's grandmother and grandfather. The grandfather's story of the incident is based on the fact that a drawbridge in Holland isn't raised because the boat scheduled to pass is upriver, leaking. If the boat hadn't leaked and the bridge had been raised, the grandparents, according to the grandfather's story, would never have met, never married, never migrated to East Chicago. Of course, the character herself, as Barrie points out, would have not then been born. There are wonderful place names that Barrie pronounces, then tutors— "No, like *this*." The towns facing one another across the Dutch river are *Heusden* and *Wijk*, the river and bridge, *Haringvleet*. The turn in Vreuls's story is that the grandmother, near her end, says that she and her husband had met in Chicago, *not* on an un-raised bridge in Holland. The grandfather, predeceasing his wife, is unavailable to comment. The grandfather said he'd been hear-ing opera in his head the day he crossed the Haringvleet to meet his bride. If the character in the story had wanted to believe her grandfather, then so had I. But asks Vreuls in her story: *Can we believe the stories of men who listen to opera?*

Therapist: the dream's recurred?—this dream?

it's a dream, or it's not. Vreuls wrote a good book I admire, *Let Us Know*. For English speakers, Dutch is the simplest foreign language to learn. The French word for wooden shoe is *sabot*, pronounced *sa-boh*. Near the turn of the century in northern Belgium, displaced farm workers would steal into the fields at night to destroy the machine harvesters that had taken their jobs. One of the principal methods of ruin was for the workers to throw their wooden shoes into the harvesters' internal works so that when the machines were cranked they would self-demolish: *sabotage*. The Japanese word for *iris* is the same as the word for *bravery* which is the same as the word for *victory*. Ancient Japanese warrior armor is covered with the images of flowers. I see myself as a man who holds his life in his hands more like argument than history. I feel unweaponed—stripped, judged. No, let's see—*resentful, anointed, unanointed, toxic, remorselessly sane, hooped, galled, expertly cored, seduced, unbreasted*.

Therapist: what are you up to? What is this?

hoarding

Therapist: hoarding?

words, *mots, paroles*, stockpiling—*hoardpiling*. My father used to quote Max Lerner about Joe McCarthy: *The crime of book purging is that it involves a rejection of the word. For the word is never absolute truth, but man's feeble effort to approach the truth. To reject the word is to reject the human search.* I like that—do you like that? Rummaged-out words are the search for truth. Otherwise, we're assembly-line parrots, cocksucking parrots. I know a woman who killed herself. When it was over, the news and all-after-hubbub—the *form* and *starch* and *wail*—the word *suicide* hardly covered it. And my father, who died of cancer, told me he started to die the second "the word shanked from the doctor's lips into my earholes. All the same, I'll tell you the word *chemo* worked for a while." My father, years dead, had it figured? Life, like a dog, if you call by its right name, will come? My father actually died before the cancer could kill him—his heart stopped and started three times, then stopped.

Therapist: you and your father—you were somewhat close then?

I knew a woman who was killed, closely related to the Shah.

Therapist: shaw? Did you say shaw?

what I think of now is how a man stood in the cold and the dark, locked out of his house. I think of how he stood in freedom before the large glass window of his locked back door—the locked storm torn off. I see the way the glass magnifies the light gushing from his kitchen. I see the light flame on his face. I see blood on his hands and on the glass-and-aluminum storm, which rocks in the snow like new sculpture. I see him shoe deep in new snow, brick of red ice in his hand, as a man with the luxury of a person with only trifles to lose.

Epilogue (cont.)

My father's people were Danes; my mother's, Swedes; and Barrie's eyes heron blue. "Our children would have been heron eyed." Virgil has heard, but lets it go.

The far-off oaks go deep. *So much happens without our help.* I have heard her clearly and close my eyes to look, but am forced to open. With my eyes shut tight I experience vertigo.

Had a friend who lost her husband young. He was an abusive sonofabitch—she was lucky he rode hog bikes drunk and bareheaded—then he died and became a saint. I said, "What are you—nuts?" I said, "You ever try to live with a saint?" What I'm saying to you is whatever we had is what we had, but don't forget that early on you sniffed out I was crazy. Don't forget that smell. Peace, lover. Pais. Pax.

The Iowa Short Fiction Award and John Simmons Short Fiction Award Winners

2001
Ticket to Minto: Stories of India and America,
Sohrab Homi Fracis
Judge: Susan Power

2001
Fire Road,
Donald Anderson
Judge: Susan Power

2000
Articles of Faith,
Elizabeth Oness
Judge: Elizabeth McCracken

2000
Troublemakers, John McNally
Judge: Elizabeth McCracken

1999
House Fires, Nancy Reisman
Judge: Marilynne Robinson

1999
Out of the Girls' Room and into the Night, Thisbe Nissen
Judge: Marilynne Robinson

1998
Friendly Fire,
Kathryn Chetkovich
Judge: Stuart Dybek

1998
The River of Lost Voices: Stories from Guatemala, Mark Brazaitis
Judge: Stuart Dybek

1997
Thank You for Being Concerned and Sensitive, Jim Henry
Judge: Ann Beattie

1997
Within the Lighted City,
Lisa Lenzo
Judge: Ann Beattie

1996
Hints of His Mortality,
David Borofka
Judge: Oscar Hijuelos

1996
Western Electric,
Don Zancanella
Judge: Oscar Hijuelos

1995
Listening to Mozart,
Charles Wyatt
Judge: Ethan Canin

1995
May You Live in Interesting Times, Tereze Glück
Judge: Ethan Canin

1994
The Good Doctor,
Susan Onthank Mates
Judge: Joy Williams

1994
Igloo among Palms,
Rod Val Moore
Judge: Joy Williams

1993
Happiness, Ann Harleman
Judge: Francine Prose

1993
Macauley's Thumb,
Lex Williford
Judge: Francine Prose

1993
Where Love Leaves Us,
Renée Manfredi
Judge: Francine Prose

1992
My Body to You,
Elizabeth Searle
Judge: James Salter

1992
Imaginary Men, Enid Shomer
Judge: James Salter

1991
The Ant Generator,
Elizabeth Harris
Judge: Marilynne Robinson

1991
Traps, Sondra Spatt Olsen
Judge: Marilynne Robinson

1990
A Hole in the Language,
Marly Swick
Judge: Jayne Anne Phillips

1989
Lent: The Slow Fast,
Starkey Flythe, Jr.
Judge: Gail Godwin

1989
Line of Fall, Miles Wilson
Judge: Gail Godwin

1988
The Long White,
Sharon Dilworth
Judge: Robert Stone

1988
The Venus Tree,
Michael Pritchett
Judge: Robert Stone

1987
Fruit of the Month,
Abby Frucht
Judge: Alison Lurie

1987
Star Game, Lucia Nevai
Judge: Alison Lurie

1986
Eminent Domain, Dan O'Brien
Judge: Iowa Writers' Workshop

1986
Resurrectionists,
Russell Working
Judge: Tobias Wolff

1985
Dancing in the Movies,
Robert Boswell
Judge: Tim O'Brien

1984
Old Wives' Tales,
Susan M. Dodd
Judge: Frederick Busch

1983
Heart Failure, Ivy Goodman
Judge: Alice Adams

1982
Shiny Objects, Dianne Benedict
Judge: Raymond Carver

1981
The Phototropic Woman,
Annabel Thomas
Judge: Doris Grumbach

1980
Impossible Appetites,
James Fetler
Judge: Francine du Plessix Gray

1979
Fly Away Home, Mary Hedin
Judge: John Gardner

1978
A Nest of Hooks, Lon Otto
Judge: Stanley Elkin

1977
The Women in the Mirror,
Pat Carr
Judge: Leonard Michaels

1976
The Black Velvet Girl,
C. E. Poverman
Judge: Donald Barthelme

1975
*Harry Belten and the
Mendelssohn Violin Concerto,*
Barry Targan
Judge: George P. Garrett

1974
*After the First Death There Is
No Other,* Natalie L. M. Petesch
Judge: William H. Gass

1973
The Itinerary of Beggars,
H. E. Francis
Judge: John Hawkes

1972
The Burning and Other Stories,
Jack Cady
Judge: Joyce Carol Oates

1971
*Old Morals, Small
Continents, Darker Times,*
Philip F. O'Connor
Judge: George P. Elliott

1970
The Beach Umbrella,
Cyrus Colter
Judges: Vance Bourjaily and
Kurt Vonnegut, Jr.

A former U.S. Air Force officer, Donald Anderson teaches creative writing at the United States Air Force Academy. He is the editor of *aftermath: an anthology of post-vietnam fiction*, *Andre Dubus: Tributes*, and *War, Literature, and the Arts: An International Journal of the Humanities*. Anderson is also the recipient of a Creative Writer's Fellowship Grant from the National Endowment of the Arts. He lives in Colorado Springs.

AND   Anderson, Donald,
       1946 July 9-

     Fire road.

$15.95

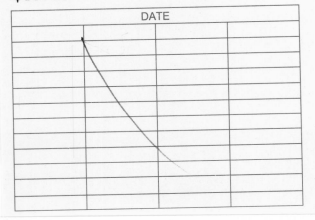

DATE			